A DAME CALLED MURDER

By
MILTON OZAKI

I0616814

ARMCHAIR FICTION
PO Box 4369, Medford, Oregon 97504

*For more information about Armchair Books and products, visit our
website at…*

www.armchairfiction.com

Or email us at…

armchairfiction@yahoo.com

ON THE TRAIL OF A SEX-CRAZED KILLER...

There was some kind of new racket in town, and private detective Max Keene decided it was in his own best interest to find out who the big boss was. Not that he didn't care about breaking the back of an organized theft ring, but when one of the ring's gorgeous young female operatives wound up dead in a sexually charged homicide and Max got fingered, it gave him an added "incentive" to bring the killer to justice. However, standing in the way was a seemingly endless maze of mis-turns and half-clues, all interwoven with a long parade of low-life characters. What Max Keene hadn't expected, though, was to be smitten by the charms of two young showgirls—a calypso-dancing redhead and a cute blonde with a snake for a dancing partner. The big question was, could he keep them alive long enough to find out what they knew...

POLICE LINEUP:

MAX KEENE

He was one of those private eyes who seemed a little shady but always played the straight and narrow. Well…most of the time.

SERGEANT HALLORAN

There weren't too many cops around who seemed as moralistic as Halloran—but what was his connection to a young show girl?

GWEN COLLYER

She was a dreamy-eyed redhead and a wannabe calypso dancer who found a private eye lying in her apartment—unconscious!

SERGEANT NEHLSON

He was a tough vice cop with a good reputation, but somehow Keene thought there was more to him than meets the eye.

SALLY BREEZE

This gorgeous young dame was a nightclub dancer by trade, but she was a good kid—even if her dancing partner was a snake!

JIM BARONE

Max's attorney pal who had an office just down the hall. He always had a legal writ ready for whatever the situation called for.

SOLLY FRANKS

Nobody told this sleazy talent agent what to do—except for a mysterious voice on the other end of the telephone…

HELEN PARREO

This great-looking young dame was a cafeteria cashier by trade—but she handled a lot more than the customer's money.

GLOSSARY OF UNDERWORLD JARGON AS USED IN THIS BOOK

ACE—A one-year jail or prison term.

AIREDALE—One fawningly loyal, as a dog to a master.

THE BAKER—The electric chair.

BANGSTER—A drug addict who uses a needle.

BOOSTER—A thief who steals merchandise from stores.

CAMP—The flat used by thieves to hide loot, fugitives, etc.

DANGLER—Any piece of jewelry which dangles free, as an earring, pendant, etc.

DOOR-MATTER—A very petty thief, as one who would steal a door mat.

EARIE—Eavesdropper; stool pigeon.

FAGIN—One who instructs or entices youths to crime.

FEELER—A person who scouts out people or places to be robbed by others.

GASSY—Talkative.

GHEE—Guy; any male person.

GLOM—Grab, as in stealing.

HIPSTER—A smart underworld frequenter.

ICE—Gems of any kind, particularly diamonds, but also jewelry set with gems.

ICE HOUSE—Jewelry store or jewelry counter.

JAMMED UP—Arrested; in serious trouble.

KISS-OFF—Any tactic to rid oneself of the victim of a theft without giving offense or attracting attention; also to rid oneself of unwelcome company without giving offense.

LAMESTER—One who has jumped bail, escaped from prison, or in any manner is a fugitive from justice.

LIFT—Steal.

LIVE ONE—A sucker with money.

MAC—A pimp; a loafer supported by a working girl.

M. O.—Modus operandi; the mechanics of a crime.

PADDED—Having stolen goods secreted on one's person.

PEE-WEE—A stupe; a person of little brains or negligible status.

RICHARD—A detective or plainclothesman; a variant of dick.

SHAKE—The initial theft or swindle; successive thefts are bites or rehashes.

SHARPIE—One who knows the angles of a racket.

SINKER—A thief who withholds a portion of the loot, thus cheating his accomplices.

SOCKO—Terrific; the best; a smash hit.

UNCLE—A buyer of stolen goods; a pawnshop proprietor.

WASHER—Coins; small change; a trivial sum of money.

YARD AND A HALF—$150.00.

CHAPTER ONE

MAX KEENE eyed the front of the Handy Andy Cafeteria rather dourly, then he spat into the gutter, crossed an expanse of sidewalk, and jerked back the chrome-trimmed door.

Business had been smelling mildly all month, a not unusual occurrence in August, and Max had resigned himself to putting in a week or two of time on a checking job he handled for the Handy Andy Corporation on an annual fee basis. It wasn't a large account, but the fee came in regular quarterly installments without much prodding on his part and he didn't want to lose it, even though the work was distasteful. The Handy Andy Corporation, operating a chain of widely patronized cafeterias in Chicago's busy Loop, realized its cashiers and managers were merely human and subject to the usual temptations. So it was deemed wise to have a trained, impartial eye scrutinize their activities at regular intervals.

The work consisted in the main of Max's dropping in for a meal at one location and another, guzzling too many cups of coffee, and adroitly stalling long enough to observe the cashiers and managers in action. Later, he would tail them home to make certain they rode a bus and not a Cadillac, then he would check their residences against the ones recorded on the personnel lists. Occasionally he would even prowl their apartments to make sure their shopping habits hadn't suddenly switched from State Street to Michigan Avenue. It was a job that always sent twinges of disgust through Max Keene; but a private eye learns to pluck fees wherever he can… And, actually, it was amazing how often a cashier succumbed to the lure of an easy buck!

He had hit three units already that morning and his kidneys were sloshing around in a bellyful of coffee. But, suppressing a sigh, he entered the cafeteria, walked to the automatic check dispenser and snatched a pasteboard ticket from it. The dispenser chimed softly and the cashier's eyes flicked toward him. She was a pert little thing, somewhere in her early twenties, with dark curly hair and little make-up. She wore a rather cheap, frilly blouse, white, the kind featured in department store sales; and over the blouse a close-fitting black cotton jumper. The jumper, although obviously inexpensive, was effective. It molded her curves snugly and, as she twisted and turned on her stool, deftly spindling checks, manipulating the register, reaching for packs of cigarettes, counting out bills, and sweeping change into the drawer before her, the front of the jumper undulated busily. So busily, in fact, that, for an instant, Max felt a subtle sexy sensation, as if a bad fairy had stroked him with a magic wand.

He got a tin tray and pushed it slowly past the racks of pastries, salads, fruits, and gravy-soaked meats, keeping his eyes at the job of adding and subtracting details. The manager was a florid-faced, gray-haired guy in a white duck jacket. Max spotted him in the rear, apparently raising hell with a meek-miened girl chopping lettuce for salads. The line wasn't crowded but Max took his time, finally accumulating a roast beef sandwich, a piece of apple pie, and a cup of the inevitable coffee. A pimply-faced youth at the end of the line moved his lips silently over Max's tray, then gashed the pasteboard with a chrome punch. Max glanced at the ticket to see if the checker was on the ball. He was.

For the next half-hour, Max sat at a table that had a good view of the pert cashier. He munched desultorily on the roast beef sandwich and nibbled at the apple pie. Mentally, he kept count of the dings emitted by the check machine, the number of exiting customers, and the number of times the cashier's register went BUP-rrr. The simplest way for a cashier to rook a joint is by accepting cash from five customers, ringing up only four of the checks, and later destroying the extra check. He watched her closely, particularly when a string of customers approached the plate-glass showcase where she presided, but after a while he decided she wasn't doing anything fancy. At least, she was banging the register the proper number of times. Maybe she was a new girl and hadn't caught onto the ropes yet.

There was a lull in the stream of cash-waving patrons for a minute and, like a woman who has nearly reached the point of exhaustion, the cashier folded her arms across the open cash-drawer and rested her head upon them. After a moment she jerked her head up abruptly, as though fearing she had been observed, and her eyes, dark and somewhat tired-looking, swung around nervously and came to rest on Max.

He grinned at her, making it a friendly grin. Without hesitation, she flashed a wry smile back and jiggled an eyebrow as though to convey the information that it's a great life if you don't weekend.

The moment of communication was brief, but not too brief to make Max realize that she was a darned attractive kid—and, more sharply than ever, he felt like several kinds of heel for spying on her. A private dick gets all kinds of jobs, of course, some of them pretty mucky; after a few years of chasing deadbeats and wading through the cesspools of divorce actions, he learns to go about a job without tangling himself in a lot of philosophical abstractions. But this job stuck in his craw. She looked like a nice kid. She was somebody's daughter, was probably a small-town girl trying to make a buck in an unfriendly big city. And there he was, snooping around, trying to get something on her, so he could run to the company management and prove he was earning his fees. Guiltily, he shifted his chair and stared morosely at the food-forking customers at the tables surrounding him.

It was the usual assortment of hungry or time-wasting people that flows through any big cafeteria day in and day out. There were old men gumming cupcakes and peering at newspapers. There were harried-looking women with kids and sharp-eyed women without kids. At a nearby table, a young man was eating hurriedly, one eye on the clock and the other on the bosom of a girl at a neighboring table. Max, following the young man's trajectory, lifted his eyebrows and moistened his lips. It was a spectacular bosom, and Max, having been a bottle-fed baby, eyed it admiringly before shifting his gaze to its owner. She was a compact, well-built, well-dressed woman, in her thirties, he guessed, and she sat three tables away from him, daintily tasting a sugared doughnut and offering an excellent view of a patrician profile. She wore a burnt-orange suit of silk gabardine and a matching hat that sat saucily atop a thick coil of braided blonde hair like a cherry on a mound of lemon ice cream.

She nibbled the doughnut without much enthusiasm, as though more worried about not smearing her bright red lipstick than satisfying her stomach. While Keene's gaze lingered on her, she completed the half-hearted assault on the doughnut, sipped sparingly of the coffee, and prepared to leave. She blotted her lips with a tissue, gathered up purse and white gloves, then pushed back her chair and walked toward the cashier with the lithe, springy step of a young mare. She was about five-eight, Max estimated automatically, a nice height for a woman, and she weighed in the neighborhood of one-thirty.

He followed her with his eyes all the way to the cashier's station and saw her lay down a dollar bill and pick up her change with long slender fingers. Hardly glancing at the cashier, she dropped the change into her purse, turned, and walked toward the door. Max grinned and decided that Hogarth had been absolutely right; the S curve was a thing of beauty. She really had a beautiful S.

The door closed behind her, releasing his eyes, and he glanced at the table she had left. The glance began as a lazy reflex, but it ended in amused surprise. She had forgotten two packages, each about the size of a blouse box and wrapped in the distinctive greenish-blue paper of Shield's Emporium. He rose, impelled to run after her and call her back, then he thought...*hell, she'll be back. She can't help missing them right away.* But she didn't. Minutes passed in slow succession, the packages remained on the table, the blonde didn't return, and finally Max saw the cashier go to the table, carry the packages to a closet, and stow them on a shelf.

Something about the way she did it puzzled him. He was still puzzling when a skinny guy in a brown suit came in hurriedly and deposited a paper carton on the table that the blonde had occupied. He dropped a battered felt hat on top of the carton, hurried to the line, got a tray, pushed it down to the pastry section, and came back with two sugared doughnuts and a cup of sloshing coffee. Max stared at him, then at the doughnuts; he had about decided that the doughnut business was pure coincidence when, with obvious nervousness, Skinny Guy pushed away the remains of a doughnut, gulped his coffee, and started for the cashier, taking his hat but leaving the carton. When he approached, the cashier had her head on her arms again, but the rattling of his change on the glass aroused her. She gave him an impersonal, apologetic smile, dropped the silver into the drawer, and rang up the correct amount. Skinny Guy grabbed for a toothpick then scuttled for the door.

Max, suppressing a frown, lit a cigarette and carefully avoided staring at the carton. As before, the cashier waited a few minutes, then walked to the table, picked up the carton, and put it in the closet. Max watched her closely and decided that she was either sick or damned tired. She swung her legs as though she were forcing herself to move, and as soon as she got back to the register she rested her head On her arms again and her body trembled spasmodically, as if she were sobbing inwardly.

Max got more coffee and another piece of pie and watched her for another hour. In that interval, two other people entered with packages, bought sugared doughnuts, sat at the same table, and left without their packages. It was beginning to figure, but he still wasn't sure. It looked too pat.

He paid his check and went out, walked down the street a couple of doors, then made himself comfortable against a lamppost where he could keep an eye on the cafeteria's entrance. He watched it for another two hours, smoking innumerable cigarettes and noting that, although quite a few women entered with assorted parcels in their hands, they were startlingly forgetful and invariably left one or two of them behind. Blondie didn't return; neither did Skinny Guy. Obviously the premises of the Handy Andy cafeteria were being used as a drop by a troupe of department store boosters—and apparently the cute cashier was taking a hand in operations.

He looked at his watch. It was 2:54. The cashier would be going off duty at 3:30, but she'd probably linger for the free feed that was part of every Handy Andy employee's wages. Then she'd have to powder her nose, straighten her seams, and get the packages organized. It would take her a half-hour, he figured, give or take a few minutes. To while away the time, he walked down to State and Madison and bought a pack of cigarettes and a Daily News.

Glancing up from time to time, Max skimmed through both sections of the paper. Then he strolled back to the lamppost. It was 3:15. He pored through the paper again. At 3:55 the door of the cafeteria swung open and the cashier stumbled out, her arms loaded with packages.

Max did a quick double take, then ducked his newspaper into a trashcan and started rapidly toward her. She was looking up and down State Street as though searching for a taxi when he bumped against her, sending the packages rattling to the sidewalk. Murmuring a quick apology, he bent and began picking them up. Some were fairly heavy, some were very light and, altogether, there were an even dozen of them. The girl stood stiffly, as though stricken while he gathered them together and replaced them in her arms.

"Sorry, kiddo," Max growled, bending his lips into what he hoped was a likeable grin. "I was rushing along, thinking about nothing, I guess, and… Well, it's my fault. I didn't hurt you, did I?"

"No." There was a toneless quality in her voice.

"Hope nothing's broken," Max stretched the grin a little wider. "Say, I've a car in the parking lot across the street. Could I give you a lift some place?"

She eyed him blankly for a moment, then shrugged.

"Sure."

The blank look was like a pan of cold water in his face. He was pushing forty and getting a little gray around the edges, definitely no longer the virile, bouncy type that made young girls break into a sweat; but he had good shoulders, a full head of hair, only a slight paunch, and a round, honest face. He hadn't expected her to sizzle at his flip invitation, but he felt that he rated something more than dull resignation.

She walked beside him in silence to the parking lot, clasping her armload of packages against her white wool jacket. When he helped her into the car, she dropped them in a careless heap on the seat, then leaned her head against the seat cushion and closed her eyes. He walked around his Pontiac and climbed behind the wheel, trying to shake the memory loose. As he fitted the key into the ignition, he noticed that her eyes were still closed and that her hands were balled into tight little fists, the kind a child makes while waiting for the initial stab of a dentist's drill. He forgot the memory that had been nagging at him and thought, *She's no dummy. She knows she's been spotted. Bet she's getting an act ready.*

Aloud, he asked, "Where do you live, kiddo?"

Hardly moving her lips, she murmured an address on East Chestnut.

He repeated it, then asked, "Got a name?"

"Helen."

"Glad to know you, Helen. My name is Max." He flashed another grin at her. "Max Keene—and don't ask me if I'm sharp, because most of the time I'm not."

The corny crack got no rise from her and, while he drove north on State Street, he mentally considered ways and means of telling her that the Handy Andy Corporation had an aversion to employees who dabbled in illegal activities; that it was his job to report that she had been helping a crew of boosters unload their loot on the premises of a Handy Andy cafeteria. There would be screams of protest and a flood of pseudo-innocent tears, he surmised, but he'd be a hell of a private cop if he didn't slap the dirty end of the stick at her and make her hold still. She was as much of a crook as the troupe she was helping. The thought didn't make his cup runneth over, but he made up his mind to do his duty and put a quick, painless period to her career as a Handy Andy cashier. Later he could get a few scotches and forget the whole damned mess.

At Chestnut Street he swung east and drove slowly until he spotted the number. It was a large frame building, newly painted white, which looked as though it had once contained eight large flats but had recently been converted into small, more profitable kitchenette units.

"Well, here we are, kiddo!" he announced, parking his car.

She opened her eyes reluctantly and stared at the building. "So we are," she murmured. Her hand fumbled for the door release.

He got out, went around the car, and opened the door. He offered her his hand and she clutched it with cold fingers, swung her slim legs to the ground and, clutching his hand tightly, and stood erect. Ignoring the packages, she started up the walk, stumbled, caught herself, then moved toward the building entrance with an odd, weary gait. She reached the doorway, lurched slightly, and banged her shoulder against the wooden jamb. As Max ran toward her, her purse fell from her hands and a small moan escaped her. He slipped an arm around her, holding her on her feet, and bent to pick up the purse. Beneath the wool jacket, she was trembling violently. He got the purse open and found a brass hotel-type key stamped with the numerals 209. It fitted the outer lock. As the bolt shot back, he pushed the door open.

"Thanks," she muttered. "I'm okay."

"Can you stand here a moment?" Max asked. "I'll get your packages."

She squeezed her eyes shut, as though enduring a spasm of pain, then leaned against him and went limp in his arms. He held her awkwardly for a moment, like an unwilling lover, his mind chewing over the problems brought on by the unexpected situation. Her eyes were closed and small bubbling gasps were coming from her throat. Max peered into the building. The foyer was deserted. Making up his mind, he kicked the door shut, swung her up into his arms and headed for a linoleum-covered stairway that led upstairs.

She moaned and bit her lip when he shifted her to unlock the door of 209, then went limp as a wet rag as he carried her into the apartment. In the semi-gloom he located a rumpled studio couch and carried her to it. She was gasping for breath and writhing as though in great pain. He snapped on lights and stared at her skeptically, more than half convinced that she was putting on an act in an attempt to delay the verbal blow she knew it was his job to administer. But if this was an act, it was damned good; in fact, it was too damned good. She was in pain. Suddenly convinced, he knelt beside her and laid a hand against her forehead. It was feverish and moist with perspiration.

"Hey, kiddo," Max growled, "what's the matter? You really sick?"

At the sound of his voice, she opened her eyes wildly, clawed at the couch and swung her legs to the floor. With a choking sob, she got up and tottered through a doorway into another room. Considerably perplexed, Max stood up and listened to the sound of stumbling footsteps and the rattle of haphazardly opened drawers. When she reappeared in the doorway she had taken off the white jacket. There was a crazed glint in her eyes, and a gleaming automatic of small caliber in her right hand.

"You fool!" she began in a frenzied voice. "Oh, you damned foo—!"

As the gun began to rise, Max reacted automatically. He sidestepped quickly, then leaned toward her, cutting the edge of his hand down across her wrist. The gun made a snapping sound, like that of a small dry twig breaking, and he felt a hot streak sear the length of his arm. Then his hand struck her wrist and the gun clattered to the floor. A scream began to rattle in her throat, climbing loosely like a soprano on a radio set that has a defective tube. Still reacting automatically, Max slapped her across the mouth, stopping the scream in mid octave, then caught her arm and jerked her forward. She came into his arms like a chunk of ice sliding into a bucket. He held her tightly a moment, expecting her to try to fight free, but she was completely relaxed and he could feel the spasmodic throb of her breasts beneath his arms. He hesitated, then swung her off her feet and tossed her onto the couch. She choked back a scream, rolled her head from side to side, and moaned softly.

Cursing inwardly, Max hurried to the kitchenette section where a small sink and a refrigerator huddled cosily together. He turned on the cold water faucet. While searching in a cupboard for a glass, he spotted a half-empty bottle of Vat 69. He poured a generous slug of the liquor into a jelly glass and hurried back to the couch. Her lips were as taut as wet canvas and as colorless. He held the glass against her mouth. She twisted her face away. He got an arm under her, held her against his chest, and forced the edge of the glass between her lips. She gagged and choked and rolled her eyes loosely, but some of the liquor went down. As he stood up, holding the empty glass in his hand, she shuddered violently, then sighed and lay still.

A cold hand closed over his heart. "Hey, kiddo!" Max cried hoarsely.

She didn't move.

Disbelievingly, he pulled down the bib of the black jumper and unbuttoned the top buttons of the nylon blouse. He laid the palm of his hand between the cleft of her breasts and discovered that her pale skin was smooth and warm and very moist. He held his breath, waiting for a faint rise of breathing, praying for a slight throb of pulse. It seemed minutes before he detected her slow heartbeat, then felt the rise and fall of her lungs. She had fainted. She wasn't dead.

Relief began to swirl through him—and then he sensed someone behind him. As he started to turn, the ceiling rapped him on the head and the unconscious girl's arms seemed to reach up and clasp him.

CHAPTER TWO

HE REGAINED consciousness with the deep-seated conviction that his head had been pounded with a stapling gun. When he tried to open his eyes, sharp tines of pain stabbed through the lids, sending flashes of agony into his head. He licked at his lips and groaned. Somewhere in the wide black yonder a voice said, "Oh, so you aren't dead."

He groaned again and tried to concentrate on small things like breathing regularly and knowing where his hands and legs were. Gradually his senses sharpened. He was sprawled face down on a floor and his nose was poking into a dusty carpet. He moved his head a little trying to un-squash his nose. Instantly a flame leaped through his skull. He jerked his head violently and felt the floor heave beneath him. Gradually the flame died down. He was on his back now. He realized, vaguely, that someone had rolled him over. That reminded him of the voice. So he wasn't dead. This was some other kind of hell.

The voice said, "Here, try a slug of this."

A hand pressed his chin, forcing his jaw open. A liquid trickled into his mouth. He choked and gasped, then the life giving fumes of a good whisky seeped into his nostrils and he sucked thirstily and noisily at the trickle until it ceased.

"Don't be a pig," the voice advised.

The liquor swirled into his stomach, loosening his reflexes, and he got his eyes open. A room wobbled around him and a face swam into focus. It was a woman's face, surrounded by a halo of copper-red hair and containing eyes the shade of gunmetal—and as hard. He closed his own eyes a moment, then opened them again. She was still there. He tried to sit up.

"Don't try any tricks," she warned pleasantly. "If you do, you'll stop being a boy."

He noticed, then, that she held a short-barreled revolver in her right hand and that the gun was pointed at him. He also noticed that she was dressed in a cream-colored knitted dress that showed everything except her appetite and that she was built like a boy in the places that don't count and very much like a girl in the places that do. While he stared at her, she lifted a glass she had been holding in her left hand, toasted him with it as though he were an old friend, then drained it and set it on the polished top of a console record player.

"If you can talk," she said in the pleasant tones, "you might explain what the hell you're doing in my apartment."

Max tongued his lips, then rasped, "Where am I?"

"So that's your line." She twisted her lips into a scornful smile and moved the gun in a way that made his heart thump like a rug-beater against a dusty carpet. "There seems to be a lot of screwy business going on in this building today," she went on, watching him through slitted eyes. "When I came in, there were two squad cars out in front and a lot of heat was running up and down the stairs. Then I find you, out like a light, cluttering up my parlor. I don't mind excitement, but I'm getting sort of nervous. Unless somebody starts explaining things, my trembling finger might accidentally tickle this trigger."

"My name is Max Keene."

"Old Maxie Keene, huh?" Her voice was derisive. "And who the hell are you, Maxie?"

Max wondered himself, but he growled, "I'm a private dick."

"No kidding." She eyed him with increased interest. "You look like too big a boy to be sneaking around following people. Where's your badge?"

"Nuts." Max frowned his disgust. "Private cops don't wear them."

"Then how do I know you're not snowing me?"

"There's a card in my wallet, a state license with my picture and everything," he growled sarcastically.

"And where's your wallet?"

"In my jacket." He started to move his hand but a quick movement of the gun froze his arm against his side.

"Don't move," she warned. "We can check the wallet later. How'd you get in here?"

"How would I know? Somebody slugged me."

"Probably served you right. Who were you following?"

"No one."

"How'd you get in the building?"

"I came in with a girl."

"Oh." She lifted an eyebrow. "The girl who got killed?"

"Who said anybody's been killed?" he asked pointedly.

"One of the coppers. A girl named Helen Parreo. Lived a couple of doors down the hall." She eyed him with the studied blandness of a person approaching the punch line of a dirty joke. "I got a hunch you killed her. What are you, a sex fiend?"

"For cryin' out loud," Max rasped, a hurt tone in his voice, "do I look like I have to get it like that?"

"Could be." She pursed her lips, frowned thoughtfully, and began to move the muzzle of the gun in idle little circles.

"Look, kiddo," Max said apprehensively. "How about pointing that rod somewhere else for a while? I'm a legitimate private dick. I can prove it."

"Maybe you're trying to trick me."

"With the building full of heat?" he asked sarcastically. "Let me get up so I can at least find out what's going on."

"I'll tell you what's going on. They're carrying her out to the dead wagon. Any minute now, they're going to go through the building, pounding on doors, questioning everybody about the sex fiend who killed her." Her gray eyes flicked toward the door. "They'll be here pretty quick and I'm going to have to come up with some kind of a story. I'll bet if I shot you I'd get a lot of publicity."

"A lot of good it would do you!" Max growled.

"Publicity is publicity," she retorted, "especially in my business."

One thing about a private dick, he learns to develop a quick eye for an open hand and a supersensitive ear to a motion to fix. Max stared at her a moment, then asked, "What's your business?"

"Not what you're thinking, but don't think I haven't had offers." She eyed the gun in her hand. "If you're a private dick, you ought to have a gun. How come you aren't carrying one?"

"I didn't expect to walk into a rat nest."

"Be prepared, that's my motto. Learned it when I was a Girl Scout," She weighed the gun in her hand, and eyed him quizzically. "As I was saying, this gun could solve a lot of your problems. Right?"

Max, catching the subtle suggestion in her voice, relaxed a bit. "Sure," he agreed. "Maybe you ought to give it to me."

"Give?" She clicked her tongue chidingly. "Hasn't anyone ever told you about women?"

"Okay." Max braced himself for the bite that he knew was coming. "How much do you want for it?"

"That's better." She nodded with the frank pleasure of a teacher with a pupil who has finally managed to come up with the right answer. "I'm not greedy," she went on, managing to sound faintly apologetic, "but things have been tough lately and it's really a very good gun. Had it around for years. In fact, I'm rather attached to it and—"

Max interrupted irritably, "How much?"

"How about half a grand?"

Max grunted. "Fire away," he advised.

"Well, maybe that is kind of steep," she admitted. "How about three C's?"

"There was about forty bucks in my wallet before I got slugged," Max said bluntly. "There may not be a dime in it now, but you're welcome to what I've got."

"I need three C's pretty badly." Her white teeth glinted as she bit her lip. "Couldn't you write a check?"

Max sniffed. "You like to watch things bounce?"

"Haven't you any friends?"

"Sure." Max shrugged. "Lots of them."

"Well, I've got a phone. You could call them and borrow the dough."

"My friends are like yours. They're broker than the Fifth Commandment."

"Hell." She bit her lip again, then tossed her head, making her red hair shimmer like a copper halo in the room's soft light. He realized suddenly that she was quite young, exceptionally pretty, and that the tough line she had been handing him was largely a pose.

Ignoring the gun, he raised himself to a sitting position and asked, "You in show biz?"

She tipped her head a little and narrowed her eyes. "Sort of. Why?"

"You've been putting on quite an act. What do you do...Sing, dance, or strip?"

"I do a calypso thing."

"Where?"

"Well...I haven't been here very long."

"So you're starving, huh?" Max nodded wisely, remembering the scores of other young girls he'd run into who'd come to the big city for a glittering career and who had ended up laying their ideals and pretty bodies on the line for peanuts. "Anything for a buck or to attract attention. Who's agenting for you?"

"Nobody."

"No wonder you aren't working."

"I don't need an agent!"

"You don't need to eat either," Max said bluntly. "Look, kiddo, it takes more than talent to get a job. This is Chicago, not East Lynn. In a big city, agents control all the acts that go into the joints. Even if a joint thought your act was great, it wouldn't dare hire you; if it did, their other acts would get jerked off the floor and they'd whistle a long time before any other talent would be permitted to sign with them."

"But they'd take ten percent of everything I earned!"

"How much is a hundred percent of nothing?" Max asked. "It's better to give an agent a bite than to starve to death, isn't it? Without an agent you might as well go back to LaCrosse, Wisconsin, or get a job rustling grub in a drive-in."

"Kansas City," she corrected, making it sound like eczema.

"It adds to the same thing."

"But I don't know any agents."

Max grinned. "I do."

"You mean you'll get me an agent and a job."

"Just an agent. Maybe he'll get you a job, providing your act isn't a clinker."

"How do I know you aren't stringing me?"

"You, of course, are a Girl Scout with merit badges for honesty." He didn't bother to keep the sarcasm out of his voice.

She frowned as though attempting a difficult mental calculation, then shrugged and laid the gun aside. "I guess it's six of one and half a dozen of another. But I'm a mean woman when crossed. If you don't keep your word, you're going to wish I'd shot you."

"Natch." Max got to his feet and massaged the back of his head gingerly. According to his watch it was 5:20 and judging by the sounds that penetrated the door, a brigade of cops were parading up and down the corridor. "Tell me about the girl who got killed," he said. "Did you know her?"

"I talked to her once, down in the basement. She was down there using the washing machine."

He went to the window and stared out. A gray ambulance was parked in front of the building, its rear doors open and waiting. On each side of the street, several straggling clusters of wide-eyed spectators were gaping toward the building. As he watched, two uniformed cops came out and cleared a path for a sheet-covered wicker basket, which a pair of perspiring attendants were lugging. The attendants swung the basket into the ambulance, slammed the doors, then waved to the cops and climbed into the front. As quietly as a bird leaving a bough, the ambulance slid away from the curb and headed east. He turned away from the window, feeling empty and shaken. The redhead hadn't been lying. Helen Parreo was dead.

"You knew her, didn't you," she said shrewdly.

"Briefly," he admitted. "But not long enough to learn her name."

"In case you'd like to know mine, it's Gwen Collyer."

Max nodded absently and looked around the apartment. It was a standard gouge-the-transient set-up with pseudo-modern furniture and a lot of cheap pastel upholstery. On a glass cocktail table near a plaid-covered couch, a tower of Pisa-ish pile of Variety and Billboards lay, mute evidence of the stuff of which Gwen's dreams were made. Draped carefully across a chair, a rhinestone-studded gown billowed and glittered. A telephone sat on a small corner desk, watched over by a cheaply framed portrait of a callow-faced Marine.

"My brother," she supplied. "He's a sergeant now."

"How long have you lived here, Gwen?" Max asked.

"Five months next Tuesday." She moved her shoulders carelessly, then added, "That's when the rent's due."

"Live alone?"

"So far."

"Who lives across the hall?"

"A cute boy with wavy blond hair and a Ford convertible. His name is Nickie something and he plays classical records on a loud phonograph and gives lots of parties." She wrinkled her nose fleetingly.

"What's his racket?"

"How would I know?"

"You said he gave lots of parties."

"Sure, but they're mostly for other cute boys."

"How long has he lived there?"

"A couple of months, I guess. He and Helen Parreo moved in at about the same time."

"Ever see them together?"

"Are you kidding? She had a boy friend who would have tied him in knots. A big guy, built like a wrestler. He used to come and take her out two, three times a week."

"Know his name?"

"No. I'm not the nosy type."

Max grunted and walked to the door.

"Going some place?" she asked. There was a note of disappointment in her voice.

"I'll see you later," Max promised. "I've got to talk to the cops and find out what happened."

"You're forgetting your gun." She came toward him, holding the short-barreled revolver in the palms of her hands as though it were a Christmas box of cigars. "You bought it, didn't you?"

He stared at the gun, then took it, weighed it in his hand, and made certain the safety was on. "Okay, it's a deal," he said gruffly. He dropped the gun into the side pocket of his jacket. "Your number is in the directory, isn't it?"

"Sure. Gwen Collyer. Two l's and a y."

"I'll talk to an agent I know. He'll probably call you tomorrow."

"Tell him I'm terrific, will you?"

"Why not, kiddo, why not?" He left her standing in the doorway and walked down the corridor to 209. The door was ajar. He stood in front of it a moment, wrestling with his conscience, then he tapped on the panel and pushed it open. Sergeant Zike Halloran, attached to the downtown homicide detail, swiveled his head around and glared. As he recognized Max, his glare turned into a frown, which corrugated his forehead like a torn strip of wet, cardboard.

"What the hell are you doing here, Keene?" he demanded.

"I've been visiting down the hall," Max said casually. "I heard the wagon out front and wondered what happened."

The apartment was pretty much the way he remembered it, but the girl's prone body was no longer stretched on the rumpled couch, of course. A chalked outline marked where she had lain. Near the top of the outline there was a large irregular blotch, shaped somewhat like South America.

"A girl got it," Halloran growled. "Landlady heard a crash and put in a call."

Feeling Halloran's eyes watching him, Max walked closer and stared at the blotch. Blood. But she hadn't been wounded; there had been no blood. His throat suddenly felt sandpapery. He forced himself to face Halloran.

"Somebody shoot her?" he asked.

Halloran was a big man, weighing close to two-fifty, and, like a lot of big men, he dressed sloppily and gave the impression of mental indolence. But Halloran was a smart cop with the reputation of having nailed more killers than any other man on the force. Max knew that any bulling he did would have to be done expertly or Halloran would be on him like a load of concrete.

"Knife," Halloran said succinctly. He traced a curved line across the front of his throat. "Who were you visiting?"

"Gwen Collyer, the redhead in 215." Max moistened his lips. "Any idea who did it?"

Halloran was consulting a notebook. "Hmm…Gwen Collyer. Came in at 4:55 alone. How'd you get in?"

"I was in her apartment," Max said glibly.

"What time did you get here?"

"Around four. Gwen was late."

"When did you start playing around with redheads?"

"Hell, a guy's got to try everything, doesn't he?" Max winked broadly.

Halloran snorted. "Hear anything?"

"If you mean screams or fighting, no."

"See anybody?"

"No."

Halloran snorted again and shifted his legs. Max noticed that there were powdery splotches on the smooth surfaces of the furniture and realized that Halloran's men had been dusting for fingerprints. The realization was like a punch in the guts. Involuntarily, his eyes swept the room, searching for the jelly glass and whisky bottle. They were probably already on their way to the police lab—and his prints were sure as hell on them.

"She was a nice kid," Halloran was saying angrily, as though checking off items in his own mind. "Good looking. About twenty-two or twenty-three, I'd say. Came here from

Whitefish Bay in Wisconsin about six months ago. Worked as a cashier in one of the Handy Andy cafeterias downtown. Used to be a dancing instructor at the Fred Arthur studios, according to the building's manager. Always minded her own business, didn't make trouble for anyone. I'll get that bastard who killed her if it's the last thing I ever do."

"Got any leads?" Max asked.

"A cop is supposed to short-circuit his emotions so they won't interfere with his work," Halloran went on grimly as though he hadn't heard Max's question, "but this sort of perverted sex job makes me want to puke. If I had the bastard here now, I'd tear his guts out."

"Sex job?" Max croaked.

"You should have been here, Keene. I thought I was tough enough to stand anything. God knows I've run into plenty of blood and gore since I've been assigned to Homicide. But what happened to this kid makes me ashamed of belonging to the human race. She was a sweet young girl, ripe for marriage and a home and babies, but some bastard had to go off his rocker and kill her in what must have started as a sadistic frenzy. He tore her clothes off and beat her. Her whole body was a mass of bruises. Then he cut her throat, probably because she started screaming. But that wasn't enough. After she was dead, the fiend bit her shoulders!"

"After she was dead?"

"According to the doc." Halloran balled his big hands into fists. "The killer apparently is a beast during the actual act, but he's cunning enough after the wave of insanity passes. He didn't leave a hell of a lot for us to work on."

"Tooth marks?" Max managed hoarsely.

"Sure, but they won't help worth a damn until we've got him." Halloran stared at the chalked outline on the couch. "She probably met him somewhere after she left the cafeteria and he talked her into bringing him here. Maybe she knew him before; maybe she didn't. He must have looked and acted like a nice guy—until he got her alone. Thank God she was unconscious through most of it. When I get the bastard, I'm going to see that he gets a taste of his own blood."

"Hell!" Max muttered. A picture of awful clarity had been building up in his mind: Halloran questioning Gwen Collyer. Halloran getting the B. of I. reports and matching his prints with those on the jelly glass and liquor bottle. Halloran spotting him as having been hanging around the Handy Andy cafeteria. Suddenly Max remembered something else; that automatic she'd waved so wildly had gone off alongside his arm. He'd felt the streaking bum of the bullet, so it must have ripped through the sleeve of his jacket. The hole, the powder bums...they'd be all the physical evidence Halloran would need.

Halloran gripped Max's arm suddenly and swung him toward the door.

"Let's get out of here," Halloran said violently, "before I throw up. Sometimes I wish to God I wasn't a cop."

Max stood in the corridor while Halloran locked the door, then preceded the police officer down the stairs. A uniformed cop stood in the foyer, watching the street entrance. Halloran nodded shortly to him and pushed the door open. Max walked past him through the door, intensely conscious of the sleeve of his jacket and wishing there were some way he could rip it off and instantly destroy it. Halloran, breathing a little heavily, strode beside Max until they reached the curb, where a squad car was parked.

"Want a lift?" Halloran asked gruffly.

"Thanks, Sarge." Max pointed at the Pontiac. "I've got my bus."

Max opened the door of his sedan and climbed behind the wheel. The packages, he noticed, were gone. He was fitting the key into the ignition when a screech split the air and a thin hag of a woman in a flowery housedress ran down the stairs of a building across the street.

"Officer! *Officer!*" she screeched in a voice like brittle glass. "There he is! He's the one went in with her! Don't let—"

Max's muscles froze. He stared stupidly at the screaming, arm-waving woman. So did Halloran. Then the engine of the Pontiac roared, drowning out Halloran's enraged bellow, and, with every nerve in his body jittering like a cricket's hind legs, Max gunned away from the curb and raced down the street.

CHAPTER THREE

MAYBE SOMETHING should be explained right here. A private dick, even though he is licensed by the state and carries a ticket that grants him some of the privileges of a peace officer, is not a cop. He swings no weight in the police department. In fact, most city cops hate his guts, principally because the average city cop has to pound leather for years and risk his neck every day for a lousy four grand a year, while a private dick grabs twenty-five-bucks-and-up per day for doing jobs that require little more than plain cheek and simple ingenuity. If a private dick operates on the square, he may get the grudging cooperation of the police department; but let him get caught sticking his neck out even a little and every cop in the city fights for a chance to swing the ax.

It's bad enough when a guy is a plain private citizen and gets caught in the tentacles of the law. Even if he is completely innocent, unless he has strong connections or is smart enough to make a quick motion to fix, with enough cash on hand to back the motion up, he's liable to get thrown into the maw of the police machine—which is similar in effect to being dropped into a deep well. He gets pushed and knocked from booking to questioning, from show-up to fingerprinting, from probing to hearing, from jailing to beating—and frequently it's a hell of a long time before anybody on the outside even knows that he's in the can. But it's worse if he's a private dick. Then the machine goes into high gear, grinding with exquisite pleasure, and Justice is deaf and dumb as well as blind.

Max didn't stop to rationalize all this when he gunned the Pontiac away from Halloran. He didn't have to. He reacted instinctively, knowing the dice were loaded against him and the more space between Halloran and him the better. He kicked the gas pedal down to the floorboards and kept it there until he hit State Street. Behind him, the siren on Halloran's squad car was beginning to wail. Max turned south on State, cut west on Chicago Avenue, then south again on Clark. At Ohio Street, he ran the Pontiac into an alley behind a saloon and abandoned it. Several other sirens had joined Halloran's, tipping Max to the fact that Halloran had taken time to radio a flash to the station. Every cruising squadron was alerted by now. Max walked to the end of the alley without looking back, did a zigzag for several blocks through back streets, headed without conscious thought for the rear of a Clark Street joint known as Little Harry's.

The main floor of Little Harry's was a bar. Max needed a drink, but there would be people in the bar and, at the moment, he realized that it would be smart to be fussy about whom he rubbed shoulders with. Squeezing through a clutter of garbage cans, he scaled a rickety stairway to a scarred door and pounded his fist against it. Inside someone cursed, then a chair scraped across the floor and footsteps approached. A heavy-set, undershirted man, sweating oil like a sardine, jerked the door open and peered at him through dark, heavy-browed eyes, which were as unfriendly as beetles.

"What you want?" demanded the undershirted one.

"I want in," Max snapped. He pushed past the other, nearly knocking a spread of three queens, a jack and a deuce out of his hand, before he could be stopped. There were three circular, felt-covered tables in the room, only one of which was in play. As Max burst in, five pairs of eyes swung toward him and four hands grabbed for the loose cash on the table. The fifth player was Little Harry, who was too smart to bother with quarters and half-dollars; his hand arched toward his hip. It stopped in mid-air as he recognized Max.

"What the hell, Max?" he growled. "You gotta bust in like a dose of salts?"

"Sorry, Harry. Got a minute?"

The door slammed shut. As Little Harry's okay soaked into their consciousnesses, the other men at the table relaxed, their eyes intent upon their cards in case Max's presence should turn out to be none of their business. Little Harry considered his cards carelessly, then tossed them on the table and pushed back his chair.

"Sure," he said. "This game stinks anyway."

"You got all the dough!" a thin, beady-eyed guy in a sharp pearl-gray gabardine shirt protested.

"No competition," Little Harry said easily, grinning. "You guys better learn the game."

He stood up, a huge hulk of a man, and walked stiffly toward another room, leaving his pile of money lying on the table. He turned on lights, closed the door, then waved airily at a couple of battered leather chairs.

"Still hitting the scotch?" he asked, taking a bottle of White Horse from a shelf.

"Thanks, Harry," Max said. "I could use a drink."

"Say when." He began pouring the amber liquor into a water tumbler.

When it was half full, Max said, "When."

Little Harry nodded, replaced the bottle on the shelf, then sank into a chair opposite Max. Although nearing sixty, Little Harry had the wide clear eyes of a youth and a fleshy face still as pink as a cherub's behind. The liquor slid smoothly down Max's throat, stroking his insides reassuringly. He sighed.

"Must be something big," Little Harry commented.

"I'm in a jam," Max admitted. "Where's your phone?"

Without getting up, Little Harry thrust out a long arm, scooped up a cradle phone from beside his chair. Max dialed Jim Barone's number. He was afraid Jim might have left his office, but he hadn't. As soon as he heard Jim's brisk hello, Max said tersely, "You alone, Jim?"

The line hummed a moment between them, then Jim said, "Yeah. That you, Max?"

Jim Barone's law office was next to Max's in an ancient building on the corner of Clark Street and Chicago Avenue. This fact often proved of mutual benefit. They didn't split fees, but anybody who needed a lawyer usually needed evidence checked, investigated or finagled, and vice versa. It was a good, practical arrangement because they worked hand-in-hand and trusted each other completely. Barone, in his late forties, had a bland, round face, no hair to speak of, and the reputation of being a shrewd, quick-witted lawyer. His practice was almost exclusively with the so-called lower elements of society, but Barone practiced criminal law through choice, not necessity. And as for dealing with crooks and social outcasts, whom else would a criminal lawyer deal with, anyhow? What the hell, Barone often said, they got a right to be heard, ain't they?

"Halloran of Homicide is on my tail," Max told him. "There's a good chance I'll get jugged. If you don't hear from me by nine tomorrow morning, get a writ, will you?"

"What's the trouble?"

"I stuck my nose into the wrong thing at the wrong time. You'll read about it in the papers. In the meantime, contact the manager of the Handy Andy cafeteria on State Street and find out what he's got on a girl named Helen Parreo. She's been working there as a day cashier and—"

"Helen?" Jim Barone's voice interrupted. "Has something happened to Helen?"

Max stared at the instrument. "You mean you know her?"

"Sure. She's a client."

"A client?" Max echoed. "She's a client?"

"Divorce action."

Max smiled tightly at the mouthpiece. "I have news for you, Jim. The divorce has been granted."

"Hell, the action isn't even listed for call until next month," Jim's voice protested. "Judge Healy is on vacation and he's the one who—"

"It was granted at about four o'clock this afternoon," Max interrupted. "God was on the bench."

"Make sense, Max." Jim sounded sharp and irritated.

"God granted Helen Parreo a decree of total divorcement," Max told him. "He divorced her from the human race, from taxes, and from Senator McCarthy. In other words, she's dead—and Halloran thinks I killed her."

In short, rapid, pithy sentences, because he had the feeling that time was running out, Max gave him a sketch of the situation and described the extent of his own involvement. He had reached the point where he had been slugged by a person unknown, when Barone interrupted.

"No, the proper procedure—in fact, our only legal alternative—is to get a writ of certiori from the State Supreme Court," Barone said emphatically. "That will enable us to lay the lower court's actions before a higher tribunal and gain us enough time to—"

Max grinned at the phone. "They're there already, huh?"

"Yes, exactly," Barone replied. "I'll prepare the writ and ask Judge Sebastian to sign it. It'll cost you a grand or two, of course, but that's cheap in consideration of—"

"Grand, hell," Max said, chuckling. "Don't let them push you around, Jim. I'm at Little Harry's. I'll try to call you later tonight."

When Max had hung up, Little Harry pursed his lips and folded his hands across his belly. "So you're hot?" he asked.

"Like a stripper's tassel," Max admitted. "I need some information, Harry."

"About what?" A note of caution tinged Little Harry's voice.

"You used to be a fence. Who's top man in the racket today?"

"Nobody." Little Harry pressed his lips together into a tight, straight line.

"Look, Harry. I'm not fingering anybody—and I'm not hollering cop. I'm simply in a jam and I'm trying to wriggle out." Max took another stab at the scotch, then gave Little Harry a quick picture of the passing operation he'd spotted in the cafeteria. "The way I figure it, Harry," he went on, "somebody in the deal was posted in one of the front apartments and saw me drive up with the kid. He slugged me, knifed her, then went down and helped himself to the stuff in my car. Whoever it was, he's going to make trouble for the whole string. But I want him, and I want him bad, because he's the key to the jam I'm in."

Little Harry frowned. "This is no fencing deal, Max. You're way off the beam."

"How so? I saw six or eight of them make a drop. Unless—"

"Things have changed." Harry stretched his big legs and pushed a cigarette between his lips. He struck a match, lit the cigarette, exhaled thoughtfully. "Back in the old days, a good thief could go out and grab whatever came to hand and take it to a fence," he said reminiscently. "Hell, once I stumbled onto a big house in Evanston and came out with a sack of stuff including silverware, a violin, a couple of radios, and a handful of rings and pins. I took them to a guy over on Madison Street and he gave me twenty bucks for the lot. Twenty bucks was dough in those days, so it was a pretty good deal for both of us. He could afford to store the stuff somewhere, wait until a market opened up, then unload it at a profit. But things are different nowadays. New models keep coming out. Not only that, the heat's smarter and tougher, too."

"Fences are still doing business," Max pointed out.

"Not like they used to," Harry countered. "Back in the old days, a fence usually ran a pawnshop as a front and could get rid of some of his stock that way. Customers used to hit the pawnshops regular, knowing he might be able to put them next to something good. Then the cops started the licensing routine, and now they've got a regular pawnshop detail and if uncle buys a couple of hot typewriters he's got to bury them in his back yard or file a report on them with the detail; either way, he's taking a chance of getting stuck with them. Take my word for it, there's no dough in the racket; at least, not like there used to be."

"The loot's going some place," Max insisted.

"Sure," Harry agreed. "But it's limited to certain items. Liquor, for instance, or clothing. You read about liquor trucks hijacked every day. Same with clothing. Cigarettes, too. Things like that can be peddled fast. But nine times out of ten the job is cased first, the thief knows what he's going to get, and he's got a market already lined up for it. He doesn't just grab and run, taking a chance on making a couple of bucks on the caper." Harry sucked meditatively on his cigarette. "When I was fencing, I must have had fifty grand tied up in the stuff that turned out to be junk. I used to walk up and down looking at it, wondering what in hell made me buy it. But I had to buy it, otherwise the guys working out of my stable would start switching to some other fence and I'd be out of business."

"But you got rid of it."

"By strictly a fluke," Harry assured him. "I ran into a guy who was dumber than I was and I peddled the whole mess to him for a quick ten G's. After that, I played it smarter. It's a tough racket though, no matter which way you look at it, and

I'm glad I decided to buy a joint like this. It's no gold mine, but at least I don't have many headaches. I used to have to chase my tail around town, trying to move merchandise, keeping in touch with thieves, handing out dough to contacts, dodging plainclothes dicks, watching the market, things like that. A fence had to be a damn super-salesman. Now all a fence does is walk around to the bright spots and take orders."

"Take orders?"

"That's what it amounts to," Harry smirked. "It's such a hell of a good idea I'm surprised I didn't think of it back in the old days. It works slick, the fence keeps his dough liquid, he doesn't have to lie awake nights, wondering what he's going to do with the stock piling up, and there's a minimum of risk. Even if he's tagged, he stands a good chance of talking himself out of a jolt in court. He operates like a merchant, see, only he doesn't carry around any merchandise."

"I don't get it," Max admitted. "A fence either fences or—"

"Look..." Harry sounded like a teacher addressing a not-too-bright pupil. "...suppose you want to buy a camera. Back in the old days, you went to a fence and asked him what he had in stock. He showed you what he had, and, if he was lucky enough to have what you wanted, he unloaded the camera. Nowadays cameras are too hot to handle; besides, they run to a lot of dough, and, what with all the different kinds of boxes and lenses on the market, he'd need a warehouse big as a barn and all his dough would be tied up. So he plays it smart. He doesn't stock anything. He runs into you and you tell him you'd like to buy a camera. Fine. What kind of a camera do you want? Well, you tell him you've been thinking about a Rolleiflex. Okay. What kind of a lens? You want the best, maybe a fast f.2.8 lens you'd been reading about which, with the box, lists at around three C's. The fence writes it all down and agrees to deliver it next week C.O.D., for fifty off list. Since fifty percent is a big discount, better than a legitimate dealer gets, you shake hands and it's a deal. So what does the fence do? He may not even know what a Rolleiflex looks like, but he knows a thief who's hot for cameras and he gives him a buzz. Get me a Rolleiflex with an f.2.8 lens, such and such a model, and such and such a condition, he says, and tells the thief he'll pay him thirty percent off list. That about wraps it up. The thief knows what to shoot for, everybody knows what the price is, and the fence stands to collect twenty percent simply for handling the deal.

"I'll be damned," Max said.

"It's specialization, see?" Harry said. "Like everybody else, the thieves and fences got smart and went along with economic pressure. A thief used to grab anything he could lay his hands on, but now he specializes. Maybe it's jewelry, maybe it's pictures, maybe it's surgical instruments— whatever it is, he knows nearly all there is to know about the field. And, what's more important, he knows where to unload it fast for a fair price. But the fences are nothing, just damn order-takers, and you hardly ever hear of any big robberies any more because the smartest thieves have switched to boosting," Harry pointed the tip of his Cigarette at Max. "And from what you told me about that passing operation, I'd say you're dealing with a troupe of boosters, a troupe that's working the big stores downtown. That girl was nothing but a pigeon for a sharpie on top."

"The sharpie is the guy I want, then," Max told him.

Harry shook his head. "I can't do you any good, Max. I've been out of the racket a long time."

"Put me next to a good booster," Max suggested. "Maybe I can work backwards."

"They're mostly women these days."

"I don't give a damn if they're monkeys, Harry," Max said. "I've got to square myself somehow, remember?"

Harry sucked on a tooth for a while, then smiled slightly. "You're forgetting something, boy."

"What?"

"What's in it for me?"

"Not a hell of a lot," Max admitted. He thought a moment. Harry, like most of the boys, believed that a buck in the hand was worth two in the bush, but cash money was what Max had very little of at the moment. He grinned suddenly. "Suppose I put you next to a good act for your joint downstairs?"

"What kind of an act?" Harry looked interested.

"A cute redhead who does a calypso shot. It ought to go over big."

"Who's agenting her?"

"Nobody. That's the point. She's fresh talent and it wouldn't hurt you to sign her up with Solly Franks. He'd have to give you first crack at her, and he might even be grateful enough to give you a break with some of the other acts he handles."

Harry lifted an eyebrow. "You sleeping with her?"

"I wish. She just came in from Kansas City."

Harry thought about it a moment, then shrugged. "Could be," he agreed. "Where do I contact her?"

"Her name is Gwen Collyer. I'll have her drop in tomorrow morning."

"Okay," Harry said, nodding. "The way business is, maybe a fresh act would do some good." His eyes narrowed. "I know you're okay, Max, but this has to be handled smart. I don't want any kickbacks. Understand?"

"There won't be any," Max assured him. "I told you what I wanted and you heard me talk to Jim Barone. No matter what happens, you're clean."

"Okay," Harry rolled his lip. "You'd better buy something," he decided. "You in the market for anything? A wristwatch, maybe a mink stole for your girl—"

"How about a suit for me?" Max asked. He showed Harry the sleeve of his jacket. "This one is kind of shot up."

"Yeah, a suit." Harry's eyes measured him. "A 42 long ought to do it," Reaching for the phone again, Harry dialed a number, closing his eyes dreamily while he waited for the connection. "Mabel?" he asked softly. "This is Little Harry... Yeah, same old story. How's it with you...? Yeah, with your dough I might. Look, Mabel, I got a pal here who needs a gray flannel suit, wide pinstripe, size 42 long. Can you do anything for him...? He's here now and the quicker the better. Hell, some of the stores are still open, aren't they? This is a personal favor... Okay... Sure. I'll send him over." He dropped the receiver onto its cradle. "She'll have one picked up for you. Remember, all I did was help you make the contact."

"Thanks, Harry. Did she mention a price?"

"It'll be a hundred-buck suit for half a C."

"I'll need a check cashed."

"Write it out." Harry stood up. "Anything else?"

"Get rid of this jacket for me." Max stripped it off and transferred the short-barreled revolver and all the papers in its pockets to his trousers. As he handed the jacket to Little Harry, he added, "I mean get rid of it, Harry. It could be plenty of trouble if the cops latched onto it."

"Right." Harry rolled the jacket up, took the check that Max handed him and peeled five tens off a thick wad of bills that he took from a side pocket. "Mention my name," Harry advised. "She'll be expecting you."

"Thanks much, Harry."

"That calypso babe you're sending better be damn good," Harry warned, "otherwise I'm liable to think I've been rooked."

"It wouldn't be the first time, would it?" Max asked, grinning.

"Guess it wouldn't," Harry admitted. "I'll burn the jacket."

The card room was blue with cigarette smoke and the players were slapping their cards around with the intent single purpose of rooting hogs. "Come on, Harry, get back in the game," one of the players growled. "I ain't had a decent hand since you been out."

"In a minute, boys, in a minute," Harry promised. He unlocked the rear door. As Max ducked down the stairs he heard Little Harry say, "Look, you bastards, I'm going to show you how to play cards..."

CHAPTER FOUR

THE ALLEY, filmed with the gray of fading daylight, had the pungent acrid smell of a hencoop. Max stood still for several minutes, listening to the sounds about him, then threaded a cautious path around rusting garbage cans toward Huron Street.

Max walked swiftly west to Wells Street, then north to Chicago Avenue, keeping a wary eye on the street traffic and listening alertly for the warning scream of sirens. The avenue seemed normal enough, so he turned west again, pausing briefly to feign an examination of the plaster casts of bunioned feet in the windows of the Dr. Scholl clinic while a fire insurance patrol passed. At Franklin Street, he crossed the avenue and ducked into the El station. A nickel got him an early edition of the *Tribune* and, by passing two dimes to a harried-looking old crone in a steel-grilled ticket cage, he gained entry to the train platform upstairs. The first train to appear was a Ravenswood B. He boarded it, selected a seat near a door, and leafed rapidly through the paper.

There was no mention of the killing of Helen Parreo. This puzzled him a little, for the discovery of her body must have been flashed to the City News Bureau in plenty of time to catch the early editions. The *Tribune,* though it usually eschewed flamboyant journalism, couldn't have ignored completely a story with all the circulation-building elements of a strong sex slant plus pix of a good-looking young girl like Helen Parreo. Max had expected at least a two-column headline on the front page and a photo-diagram of the killer's modus operandi in the picture section. He checked through the paper twice to make certain he hadn't skipped the story, then tossed the paper aside and swung off the train at the Fullerton Avenue station.

He still had half an hour to kill, so he strolled down Fullerton Avenue to Clark and spent a buck at a corner eatery for a portion of southern fried chicken, which tasted as though it had lain down and died voluntarily. The coffee was good, though. He drank two cups and feeling considerably bucked up, started for Arlington Place.

The address Little Harry had given him turned out to be a yellow-brick three-flat with much lawn and considerable flowerbed visible in the rear. He checked the address again, then strolled up a freshly sprinkled walk and opened a polished aluminum screen-door. There were three ebony buttons, each with a chrome nameplate. The middle plate read: *Miss Mabel Tangier.* Feeling somewhat like a slug in a handful of glistening nickels, Max pressed the proper button and waited. Almost instantly an electronic voice with feminine overtones caroled, "Who is it?" Max jerked his head around and spotted a chrome-plated grill in the ceiling above him. His nerves were vibrating like a tap dancer's fanny, but he managed to say, "Little Harry sent me." They were magic words. The voice went away, an electric release buzzed softly, and a plate-glass panel swung back, permitting him to enter an air-conditioned atmosphere. He went up deeply carpeted stairs to the second floor where an open door beckoned.

It was a swanky layout, the size of a small Sheraton ballroom, decorated in rose and gray with languid drapes, puffy pillows, billowy chairs, and armfuls of cut flowers. A slim dowager-type old lady in a yellow satin robe, which contrasted with her powder-blue hair, floated toward him across an expanse of broadloom, extending a hand in the gesture made famous by Marlene Dietrich. "Do be seated, won't you?" she trilled. "I'm sure we'll be able to take care of you in a minute."

Her hand nestled in his for a moment like a cold slice of liver, then she jerked it away and waved at a right-angled sofa which yawned invitingly in a corner of the room. The sofa didn't jump, but it did attract Max's attention and he walked to it, murmuring thanks, and sank into its foam-rubber embrace.

"We don't hear from Harry very often anymore," she went on in a tinkly voice. He noticed that she had a tricky way of tilting her head when she talked, as though she were listening to every syllable and expected them to come out dressed in ruffled organdy. "He and I used to be great friends, you know, until he moved down into that horrid Clark Street district. I've never been able to understand him! You'd think that a man with his background would want something better out of life. Why, I can remember—"

Her memories were interrupted by a double-toned chime. Flashing him a placating smile, she went to a circular grill near the door, pressed a button, and called, "Who is it?" A voice, weirdly amplified, replied, "Verne." She pressed another button, opened the door, and came back to the couch with a more businesslike vibration in her manner.

"Verne's one of our best men," she confided, gesturing with her hands like a showroom salesman extolling the virtues of power steering. "Harry didn't call until the last minute, so I was lucky to be able to catch Verne while he was still downtown. Harry explained the arrangement, didn't he?"

"He said it would be an even fifty," Max told her.

"That's right." She gave him a birdlike nod. "I do hope you like what Verne picked out." Baring her teeth suddenly she leaned toward him as though about to nibble at his ear and added, *sotto voce:* "I'll collect later. Understand?"

Before Max could reply, a tall, handsome youth with wavy blond hair appeared in the doorway. He was exquisitely dressed in a symphony of blue—medium blue suit, light blue shirt, dark blue tie—and carried a midnight-blue cashmere topcoat draped carelessly over one arm.

"Verne," Mabel trilled, floating toward him and giving him the bent wrist routine. "How sweet of you to accommodate me like this!"

"Darling, it's a pleasure!" he cried, doing something hippy. His voice fluctuated indecisively as though it was trying to make up its mind whether or not to change. "All you have to do is ask, you know that…"

"Were you able to get it?"

"But certainly, darling!" Like a magician unveiling a pair of rabbits, he swept the topcoat from his arm, unfolded it with an Oscar Wilde-style flick of a wrist, and revealed a striped gray flannel suit jacket. He hung the jacket on a chair, unbuttoned his coat, and removed a matching pair of trousers that had been pinned about his waist.

"You're sure it's a 42 long?" Mabel asked anxiously.

"Has Verne ever made a mistake?" he cried, dancing away as though offended.

"No, but there's a first time for everything." She inspected the jacket and trousers with an air of efficiency, then handed the jacket to Max. As he slipped it on, he spotted a Finchley label. She circled him, slapping at his shoulders and tugging at his lapels. It fitted well enough when he removed the revolver from his trouser pocket. Sight of the gun didn't faze her, for aside from muttering, "That's better!" she ignored it completely. Unbuttoning the jacket, she held the trousers against his waist. Frowning a little, she took a piece of tailor's chalk and a tape measure from a pocket of the yellow robe and knelt in front of him. Max stood rigid while she ascertained the proper length of the trousers. When that had been done to her satisfaction, she draped the trousers over her arm, motioned Verne to follow her, and sailed away into the depths of the apartment. Max sighed and sank back onto the sofa.

The soft clasp of the sofa and the air-conditioned silence began to act like a sedative. He closed his eyes for several minutes, but the continued silence began to gnaw at him. He got up and paced restlessly about the room, thinking about Jim Barone, about Helen Parreo, about Sergeant Halloran, and somewhat more fleetingly, about Gwen Collyer. He was at the window, staring down the street, when he heard a patter of feet behind him. Turning swiftly, he spotted Verne going out the door. Max swung his head back to the window, a sour smile on his lips, and waited for the swish to come out the front entrance and swish down the sidewalk. But Verne didn't appear. Frowning, Max waited a while longer, then crossed the room and jerked the door open. The stairwell was as quiet as an old maid's bedroom—and as empty. He closed the door and strode back to the window. He could see quite a way up and down the street, but the pretty boy wasn't in sight. What the hell?

He was still puzzling over Verne's disappearing act when Mabel returned. She tossed the freshly cuffed trousers to him saying, "Here you are. Bet they fit fine now."

"Thanks." Max glanced around pointedly. "Is there some place I can change?"

She cackled with liquid phlegm, implying that he was overly modest, but pointed at the corridor. "There's a powder room there. First door to your left."

It was a small cubicle, painted the green color of after-shaving lotion, and containing all the usual equipment except a tub. Max stripped off his slacks and stepped into the gray trousers. They fitted surprisingly well. As he emptied the pockets of the slacks, he wondered what to do with them.

They were less than a year old and had set him back twenty bucks at Field's. But he certainly couldn't carry them around all evening. He decided they were expendable and hung them on a hook behind the door for Mabel to dispose of at her convenience.

He was redistributing his possessions in the pockets of the new trousers when the mirrored door of the medicine cabinet caught his eye. Most private dicks are queer for medicine cabinets—and Max was no exception. A medicine cabinet is like a library of a household's traits and habits. Sometimes it's possible to tell nearly as much about a person by studying a bathroom medicine cabinet as it is by shaking down a bedroom.

Max unsnapped the door cautiously and stared at its narrow glass shelves. A giant economy-size tube of Colgate's dental cream, a half-empty bottle of Listerine, a large bottle of Empirin, one of the tiny razors designed for women to use when shaving their armpits, a jar of deodorant cream, extra razor blades, dental tape, a gilten-crusted flask labeled *Forest Dew,* an assortment of bobby-pins, combs, and a hairbrush with a plastic handle. Max studied the items, shrugged, and was about to close the door when the hairbrush caught his eye. He took it out and held it to the light. Several hairs were tangled in the nylon bristles. They were short and curly—but they were not powder blue. Very carefully, Max disentangled one, and studied it on his palm. Replacing the brush thoughtfully, he uncapped the gilt flask and sniffed at its contents. It had a woodsy fragrance, the kind a man might use. Obviously, a man used Mabel's bathroom on frequent occasions—but the nameplate in the lobby had read *Miss* Mabel Tangier.

When Max returned to the parlor, Mabel swept toward him and plucked at the front pleats of his trousers. "They fit fine, don't they?" she trilled. "Real professional, I'd say. How do they feel?"

"Okay." He counted out fifty bucks from his wallet and handed the bills to her. "What do you handle besides clothes?"

There was a brief, flinty silence while she checked the bills and stowed them somewhere within the folds of the yellow robe. "Oh, lots of things," she replied finally. "Men's clothes are a nuisance and we don't bother with them much. This was a favor for Harry mostly. What are you interested in?"

"Anything that might be turned fast," Max told her.

"Oh." There was a pause while she assessed and weighed his statement and, subtly, he could feel her mind shifting him from customer status to possible employee status. "You interested in peddling?" she asked archly.

Max shrugged. "I've lots of contacts."

Her nose dilated, as though she'd gotten a whiff of a bad odor. "Clark Street contacts?" she asked.

Max shook his head. "Michigan Avenue."

"That's smart." She nodded approvingly. "Michigan Avenue is loaded with suckers. You could probably do real good there. Which one of the joints do you work in?"

"I don't," Max said shortly.

Her eyes flicked toward the gun that he'd tucked into the waistband of his trousers. "Harry didn't say you were hot."

"He didn't say you were fencing, either."

Her eyes went opaque and she moved away from him with the little steps of a sandpiper retreating from sudden surf. Max reached for the gray jacket and drew it on, giving her time to see his point. She smiled suddenly and the front of the yellow robe fluttered as though a pair of birds were imprisoned beneath it. He deduced that she was chuckling. "Guess you've got me," she gasped between chuckles. "The kind of racket you're mixed up in isn't any of my business as long as you're smart enough to keep your mouth shut, and Harry wouldn't have sent you here if you weren't okay. You can't blame me for being careful, though. We've got enough trouble with heat as it is."

"You'll keep on having trouble if you do business with nances," Max said.

"You mean Verne?" Her chuckles turned into laughter. "Why, Verne's one of the best suit boosters in the business! You ought to see the routine he's got. He can waltz into a store, buy a necktie to break the ice, and come out with a couple of suits and a topcoat without any of the clerks being the wiser. Maybe I shouldn't tell you this, but he went for you in a big way. He wanted to know who you were and where you lived!"

Max told her what Verne could do.

She bubbled gleefully as though he'd described something hilariously funny, then sobered suddenly. "You're right," she admitted. "Maybe I shouldn't do business with guys like Verne. He's a good operator, but he's unstable. When a cop grabs someone like Verne they scream as though they had a tongue caught in the wringer and some day they'll pull us all into the suds. But good boosters are scarce. We've got enough business to keep a full-time crew busy, but the few girls we can get aren't willing to work. Maybe it's because there isn't much glamour to the racket."

"Suppose I got you some girls," Max suggested.

"Where?"

"Here and there. I told you I had a lot of contacts."

"Trained boosters aren't floating around looking for work."

"Hell, all women are thieves at heart," Max said, grinning. "It wouldn't be much trouble to train a few. They might even do it for kicks."

"You'd want a cut."

"Sure, why not?"

"Where would you get it?" she asked shrewdly.

"Off the top," Max told her. "A percentage of the take."

"Well—" She moistened her lips, torn between natural caution and the chance of driving a good business deal. "How much percentage?"

"Let's talk about that after I get the girls." Looking her in the eyes, he made a quick thrust in the dark. "Talk it over with the boss. Maybe he'll be interested."

It was a nice *touché*. "Oh, he'll be interested," she said quickly, "but he's going to want to know who the hell you are."

"Tell him to ask Harry."

"He's also going to want to be sure that you're not cutting in on Wally Friedl's crew. We've got sort of a gentleman's agreement."

"Wally's not the only guy with connections," Max said, making a mental note of the name. "Hell, I can get girls Wally never heard of."

"Well, it's worth thinking about. Where can I get in touch with you?"

"Leave word at Harry's."

"Who do I ask for?"

"Max." He figured he'd needled her enough, so he walked toward the door.

"Just Max?" There was a puzzled gray fog in her voice.

"Yeah." He opened the door and stepped into the hallway. "Thanks for getting the suit."

Closing the door firmly, he ran lightly upstairs to the third-floor landing. A single door gave entrance to the top flat and it was closed and locked. He descended the stairs rapidly, pausing for a moment to press his ear against Mabel's door. Hearing nothing, he went on down to the first floor. The lower flat was closed, locked and silent. There were no surplus doors, no way Verne could have scooted down to the basement and around to the back. A frown furrowed Max's brow as he pushed open the plate-glass panel and studied the nameplates. The top flat was occupied by a Mr. and Mrs. Robert Downing; the lower flat was the residence of a Mrs. Willard T. Drake. Neither name struck any bells in his memory, nor did either suggest that Verne might be a tenant of the building. Still frowning, he opened the street door and stepped to the walk. There was no alley alongside the building, nor any driveway. Verne could have slipped along the front of the building, of course, keeping out of sight of the windows above, but in order to get to the rear he would have had to hurdle a row of shrubs. Unless he had had an extremely strong yen to fondle the pretty flowers, it seemed a pointless and unnecessary exertion. Crossing the lawn, Max looked into the garden. A profusion of colorful flowerbeds and some steel lawn furniture came into view. But Verne did not.

Max had just decided to hell with Verne and had strolled back to the sidewalk when a well-stacked blonde in a bright blue dress came hurrying out of an apartment building on the other side of Arlington Place. She had a hat box—the kind supposed to be particularly useful to models—in one hand and a large white purse in the other, and she came out of the building fast as though she were late for an important engagement.

Max stared at her, first with admiration, then with astonishment. It seemed like too much of a coincidence, but she was the same height, same build, had long blonde hair in a coil on the back of her head, and there was absolutely no mistaking her beautiful S. She was the blonde he'd spotted in the Handy Andy cafeteria that morning.

She went east at a brisk trot to Clark Street, waited impatiently for the lights to change, then crossed the street and continued south to Fullerton. She kept the purse and hat box swinging and didn't pause to window-shop for a second. Max was a half-block behind her, his eyes glued to the wobblier portions of her, when she suddenly turned east on Fullerton. He sprinted after her to the corner, turned—and came to an incredulous halt. She had vanished. He spat an oath and ran east a half-block, studying the entryways of the buildings. No blondes, no blue dresses, nothing. Cursing fluently, he ran back to the corner. Either he was nuts or his eyes were playing tricks. She had certainly turned east and there hadn't been time for her to go very far, so where the hell could she have ducked?

He headed east again, more slowly and rationally this time, and hadn't gone fifty feet when he saw it. It was a narrow door, its single glass pane garishly painted to keep out prying eyes, and it bore the legend: Family Entrance. The phrase packed a bucketful of meaning and, snapping his fingers, Max looked back toward Clark Street. Suspended high above the building's glass-brick corner entrance was a huge vertical neon sign proclaiming in cardinal red: TROPIC ISLE. A smaller neon sign, fixed to flash with monotonous regularity, screamed in green: *Floor Show!* Her hat box, her hurried steps, the rear entrance and the neon signs added up to a positive conclusion: Blondie was a showgirl at the Tropic Isle.

Max walked to the corner, trying to decide if the lead was worth pursuing. There were six or eight other things he ought to be doing, and time spent on pegging the blonde might be wasted. A cruising squad car made up his mind for him. He pushed through glass doors into an air-conditioned version of a tropical climate and strode past a bamboo bar at which several couples were sipping cool drinks from sweating glasses. A glass partition separated the bamboo bar from a rattan theatre-restaurant, thereby saving any nickel nursing bar patrons twenty percent in federal taxes. Max entered the rattan area and winded his way among sparsely populated tables until he reached a square of bare flooring, which he figured might be a nightclub manager's idea of a stage. While he was picking out a chair from which he could watch, without too much strain, both the entrance and the stage, a waiter in crumpled black suit and shiny black tie appeared. Max eyed the waiter dourly and ordered a scotch.

"Will that be all, sir?" the waiter asked in a voice as brittle as a piece of ice in a glass of gin.

"One drink at a time, kiddo," Max growled.

"Yes, sir!"

The waiter stalked away, leaving Max alone with the rattan furniture, the whispering couples at adjoining tables, and the tropical twilight lighting, which was designed to induce a mood of grass-skirted abandonment. He had located the exits and the musicians and was wondering how long it would be before the show got under way, when, without warning, the lights went out and a spotlight stabbed a yellow circle on the floor of the stage. As the whispering of the couples died, a slender youth in a gleaming tux stepped into the circle and played unhealthily with his hips for a moment, waiting for undivided attention. He was a typical M. C., determinedly dramatic and stridently smutty, as full of inanities and innuendo as a sorority. Max lit a cigarette and wondered if the M. C.'s mother had ever had trouble sleeping with the lights off.

A hand placed a tall glass in front of him and poured a brimming jigger of scotch into it. It was a masculine hand, carefully manicured and, as it splashed a judicious amount of soda into the glass, a large diamond ring glinted from its little pinky. Max started to jerk his head around, but another hand squeezed his shoulder hard and a big dark-suited body eased into the chair next to him. Max looked into a round red face set into a white collar like a rose floating in a white dish.

"Hello, Max old boy!" Danny Green's voice was studiedly expansive and about as subtle as a fox in a hen house. "How's tricks these days, Max?"

"Okay, Danny." Max lifted an eyebrow. "You hustling drinks now?" The last time Max had seen him, Danny Green had been involved in a hat-checking deal on West Madison Street.

"You know me, Max." Danny smiled broadly, giving Max a flash of Chiclet-like teeth. "Personal service to an old friend. I've got a piece of this joint now."

"Yeah? How's business?"

"Lousy." Danny shrugged elaborately. "Maybe the tropic isle gimmick ain't so good."

"It's not a bad layout. How long have you been here?"

"Six months. I was looking for a spot and this looked like a happy deal, but maybe I got outsmarted. You still private dicking?"

"Why not?" Max asked. "I got to eat."

Danny nodded, then shifted restlessly as though trying to decide whether enough of the amenities had been satisfied. "Hope you're not onto one of my customers," he said at last.

"Not exactly." Max tasted the scotch. It was good. The swishy M. C. had introduced a dark-haired strip act and the band was beating out a few bars of bouncy introduction.

"The drinks are on me, Max. What's the play?"

Max, smiling inwardly, emptied the glass and waited until the waiter brought a refill. "There's a blonde in your show that I'm interested in," he said slowly.

"Which one?" Danny asked. "We got two."

"Chesty, well-built, wears her hair rolled on the back of her head," Max told him. "Came in wearing a bright blue dress and carrying a hat box."

"That's Sally Breeze." Danny wrinkled his face into an expression of mock sorrow. "Too bad, Max. You're wasting your time. Sally doesn't put out. Now if you want a doll who's broadminded and doesn't mind a good time—"

"What kind of an act has she got?"

"She does a strip, the neatest strip you ever saw, and she's willing as a rabbit—"

"I mean the other one. Sally Breeze."

"Oh, hell, Sally does a damn snake dance." Danny Green shuddered. "The first time I saw it, I had a doll with me who was flapping for sex, but after watching Sally and that damned snake of hers, I was wrecked. Couldn't do anything for weeks. I wanted to can her, but the customers get a kick out of the act, so what the hell. A buck is a buck, and I can always go outside and smoke a cigar when she comes on."

"How long has she been here?"

"Eight or nine months, I guess. She came with the joint." Danny gave Max a heavy-lidded glance. "She ain't in any trouble, is she?"

"Not that I know of. This is personal."

"Want a knockdown to her?"

"Later, maybe. I'll catch her act first."

"Suits me, Max. Don't be afraid to order up. The way we're losing dough, a few drinks more or less won't make any difference," Danny Green pushed his chair away from the table. "If I'm not out in front, tell the waiter I said it was okay. You can go through that door over there." He pointed to where an EXIT light glowed dimly. "She's got the third room on the right."

"Thanks, Danny."

"Don't mention it, old boy."

The M. C. was back with a forced line of soiled patter, then a thin blonde in a bespangled gown appeared holding her white arms out as though there were boils in both armpits. She sang liltingly in a thin voice, gradually divesting herself of the gown as she waltzed about the stage area. Max signaled the waiter for another scotch. It was getting close to nine in the p.m. and it occurred to him that Jim Barone might be wondering why he hadn't called. When he returned his attention to the stage, the M. C. was pumping his arms back and forth the way small kids imitate a train and screaming a falsetto introduction to, "...Miss Sally Breeze, the Queen of Squeeze...!" The band did a tricky fanfare, then slid into *Begin the Beguine.*

The blonde sprang into the spotlight, clad in a rhinestone-studded G-string, white skin, and a thick mass of yellow hair that hung about her slowly writhing shoulders like a yellow cape. She stood poised for a moment, a statue of undulating flesh, then began a circular Indiana-round-the-stake step that followed the slow beat of the music. A gasp passed through the audience like wind through wheat and, somewhere at the rear, a woman screamed. Max had been too busy with the blonde's curves to notice the snake. It was a huge, greenish-black thing, as thick as a loaf of rye bread, and it was slithering toward the circle of light, weaving its pointed, beady-eyed head in tempo with the increasing beat of the music.

As a trumpet wailed plaintively, the nearly naked girl kneeled and extended her arms, fingers touching the floor. The snake, moving with incredible swiftness, flowed up an arm, over her shoulders, and down across her breasts. She rose, kicking her feet against the floor to the throb of the music, with the huge snake wrapped about her waist in a tight, snug coil. There was an expression of exquisite torture on her face as she began a rhythmic parade. As the weird tempo increased, the snake uncoiled and coiled restlessly, caressing her thighs, squeezing her breasts, massaging the white body lasciviously, and she, as though carried away by the savage beat of the *Beguine,* began to stroke and pet and tease the python's fang-darting head.

Max felt sick and shaken, but he couldn't tear his eyes away from the nightmarish spectacle. Suddenly, as the naked cry of a trumpet arose, she went rigid, arms extended, eyes closed and lips apart, and the snake reared its head toward her mouth, its fangs flickering between her open lips in a kiss which seemed to weld snake and woman into one.

"What the hell!" Max muttered.

He gulped at the scotch, then pushed back his chair and got up. The spotlight had flickered out as the band crashed into its finale, but the red EXIT light still glowed. Max made his way toward it and shouldered the door open. A bare corridor stretched ahead. He went down it gratefully, wishing his guts would stop flapping like clothes on a line, and counted one, two, three doors. The third door was open. Max walked in—and immediately wished he hadn't.

"Well, well!" Sergeant Halloran growled. God at the end of the sixth day couldn't have sounded more pleased. "Come in, you bastard."

CHAPTER FIVE

MAX FORCED a grin and walked into the small, cluttered dressing room. His insides felt like loosely scrambled eggs, but he managed to get a casual note into his voice: "Hello, sergeant. Fancy meeting you here."

"You lousy shamus bastard," Halloran said tightly. He snaked a hand beneath his jacket and came out with a .38 in his fist. The barrel of the gun seemed as big as the end of a stovepipe.

"Are you nuts, sergeant?" Max asked. "Why the artillery?"

"Reach for the ceiling!"

"You're kidding."

"Like hell." There was an odd note in Halloran's voice. "Reach!" Max raised his hands shoulder high. "Press your hands against the wall and step back two paces," Halloran ordered, gesturing with his gun.

Max shrugged, turned, and pressed the palms of his hands against the plasterboard wall and shuffled his feet back until he was nearly off balance. "What the hell is this, anyway?" he growled.

"Back further," Halloran snapped, ignoring the question. "Let me see your tail."

Max sighed inwardly and complied. The position put him off balance and made him temporarily helpless. Halloran, using one hand, slapped expertly at Max's pockets, hips, thighs and chest, searching for concealed weapons and hidden objects. He relieved Max of his wallet, then located the gun in the waistband of Max's trousers. With a satisfied grunt, he plucked the gun out and stepped back.

"Okay, relax," Halloran directed.

Max stepped toward the wall, freed his hands, and straightened. "If this is some damn new—" he began.

"Shut up," Halloran said. He flipped Max's wallet open, glanced at the identification cards, and poked a finger at the bills. With a sniff, he tossed the wallet back and examined the gun. "Where'd you get this rod?" he asked.

"Won it in a bingo game," Max said sourly.

"I want answers, shamus—not wisecracks."

"What the hell difference does it make?" Max demanded. "It's my gun. I got a license to carry it. Where I got it is no damned business of yours."

"If it were your gun, you'd have it holstered," Halloran said flatly. "Only a lame-brained drugstore cowboy goes around with a loaded rod tucked in his belt. You picked this up recently. Where?"

"Look, sergeant." Max got out a cigarette and pushed it into the corner of his mouth. "I don't know what's eating you. I walk in here and you pull a gun on me. Without explanation, you call me a bastard and grab my gun and wallet. Maybe that tin shield of yours is giving you delusions of grandeur. Just because you're a cop doesn't mean that you're a little municipal Jesus. The State of Illinois says I can carry a gun during the lawful pursuit of my business. I can stick it in my pocket or poke it in my pants or hang it on my belly-button—and it's no damned business of yours." He struck a match and lit the cigarette.

Halloran colored angrily and blew out his cheeks like a rabbit trying to swallow an apple. "I suppose you don't know there's a city-wide pick-up order out for you!" he roared. "You deliberately ducked out on me and—"

"*I* ducked out?" Max simulated surprise. "When?"

"This afternoon! And don't pretend—"

"You mean on Chestnut Street?"

"Damned right on Chestnut Street! You knew—"

"Halloran, for the love of pete," Max interrupted. "You're sounding like a gangster. You walked to the curb with me; you even waved goodbye. I heard you holler at that stupid dame who ran into the street, but—"

"I was hollering at you!" Halloran's face had achieved the color of borscht and his voice was raucous with anger. "You heard me order you to stop, but you tore off like a—"

"Halloran, you're way off the beam," Max said, sounding very sincere. "I saw the old dame run into the street and I had to either gun my car or hit her. I heard you shout, but I figured you were warning her out of my way, because the old bat must have been either blind or nuts, running into the street like that, when—"

"You're a lying, double-talking son of a—"

"Say, what's going on in here?" a husky contralto voice asked. "I could hear you guys all the way down in the basement."

The fire went out of Halloran as though doused by a bucket of cold water. Max swung around and nearly bumped noses with the so-called Queen of Squeeze. She still wore the rhinestone-studded G-string, a thin veneer of body pancake, and very little else except a small, annoyed smile that was directed at Sergeant Halloran. Her long hair hung about her smooth shoulders like a heavy skein of yellow silk, half-clouding a face shaped like a smooth oval. Max moved out of her way, then took a quick, involuntary peek behind her to see if the snake was crawling along at her heels. It wasn't.

"Oh, hello, Sally," Halloran said. His voice had become as mellow as old Sauterne. "This is Max Keene. Miss Breeze."

"Hi, Max." She gave him a casual nod, reached for a flannel wrapper that looked as though it had worn itself out going around her curves, and began to work her arms into it. She did it with a minimum of movement, but Max found the operation interesting to watch. She was built big and solid, like a strong man's dream, and she had things a man could snuggle his head against and really build up to something big. Halloran, seeing Max's look, tightened his lips like a good Baptist getting a glimpse of a red-light district and glared at him.

Max grinned at Halloran and said, "I caught your act, Miss Breeze. It's got quite a sock."

"Thanks." She folded the front of the wrapper together and knotted the belt loosely about her waist. "Are you a cop, too, Max?" There was a lazy insolence beneath the husky tones in her voice, and Max got the impression that she was more than casually interested in him.

"No. I'm—"

"He's a private dick," Halloran growled, making it sound like something kiddish.

"Oh?" She gave Max a long look. Her eyes were slate-colored pools, Max noticed, the kind into which any man might be tempted to go wading. At close range, she seemed younger than she had when he'd spotted her in the cafeteria and now that he was talking to her, he had difficulty correlating her with the girl who had executed the lascivious dance with the big snake. In a mildly curious tone, she added, "What were you two fighting about?"

The question reminded Halloran of the artillery on display. Looking somewhat abashed, he returned his gun to its holster beneath his jacket and, after a moment of inner conflict, handed the other revolver back to Max. Max poked the gun into the waistband of his trousers again, grinned, and leaned an elbow against the tipped-up end of a big theatrical trunk that filled a corner of the dressing room. Sally Breeze had sat down on a stool in front of a make-up table and was watching Halloran through heavily mascara-laden eyelashes.

"Nothing to do with you, Sally," Halloran said awkwardly. "I was waiting here to see if you had time for a cup of coffee—and he walked in. I've been wanting to ask him some questions."

"The cashier of one of the Handy Andy cafeterias was killed this afternoon," Max said casually. "Too bad, too. A rather pretty, young, dark-haired girl. Worked in the cafeteria on State Street."

"The one near Madison?" She widened her eyes a little.

"Uh-huh." Max watched her—and waited.

"Why, I was in there this noon!" She said it without a trace of guile. "You don't mean the cashier who was there this—"

"That's the one," Max told her. "She went off duty at 3:30. Helen Parreo was her name."

"She was *killed?* How?"

"Some crazy bastard murdered her," Halloran said bluntly. He stared at Max a moment, then added, "I hear she was a pal of Max's."

"How terrible!" The way she said it, her exclamation could have denoted sympathy—or surprise. Max had the disquieting impression for a fleeting instant that, behind the pretty face, there was a brain running on 100-octane.

"So that's what's eating you," he said to Halloran.

"Damned right," Halloran retorted grimly. "You've got a lot of explaining to do."

"The Handy Andy Company is an account of mine," Max said carefully. "I run a check on their personnel periodically. I dropped in shortly after noon, bought a sandwich and a couple of cups of coffee, and sat where I could watch the cashier. She was new to me, so I watched her pretty closely. She was running the register okay, and I was about to give her a clean bill when I noticed something else." He paused, got out another cigarette, and lit it. "Four or five people came in carrying packages—and left them on a table. None of them came back and, as soon as they were out of sight, the cashier would walk over, pick up the packages, and stash them in a closet. It looked fishy to me, so I went outside and double-checked everybody going in and coming out for an hour or so. Three or four more went in carrying packages—and came out empty-handed. It began to figure then, so I hung around until the cashier went off duty, and when she came out she had an armful of packages."

"Is this on the level?" Halloran demanded.

Max nodded. He puffed on the cigarette a moment, giving Sally an opportunity to mention that she'd misplaced some packages herself that afternoon, but she remained silent. "At the time, I thought I played it pretty cute," Max went on. "When she came out, I walked into her and knocked the packages out of her arms. I helped her pick them up, then offered her a lift. She said okay. My car was across the street and she walked there with me. On the ride to Chestnut Street, she told me her name—and that's all she did tell me. She was feeling lousy, or sick, or was just clammed up. As a matter of fact, I didn't do much talking myself, because I was figuring a way of telling her that I'd spotted her racket and that she was an *ex*-cashier, and—"

"You figured she was handling a drop?" Halloran interrupted.

"Natch. It looked open and shut to me, and my job was to hand her a firm goodbye. She looked like a nice kid, and I hated to do it, but—well, you know. Anyway, I got her to where she lived and was about to go into my lecture, when she pulled a faint on me. I carried her upstairs, located a bottle of scotch, and poured a little of it into her. I was trying to check her pulse and breathing, when—wham, somebody clobbered me over the head. The next thing I knew, I was in the Collyer kid's apartment."

"Neat," Halloran commented. He sounded skeptical. "Damned neat."

"You mean the person who killed her was the one who hit you over the head and—" Sally began, looking puzzled.

"Probably," Max said.

"What happened to the packages?" Halloran demanded.

"I couldn't carry her *and* the packages upstairs, so I left them in my car. You were with me when I came down. The packages were gone. I don't know what the hell happened to them. Maybe the killer spotted them. Maybe somebody else picked them up. My car was unlocked."

"The poor kid!" Sally said sympathetically. "She must have been sick or she wouldn't have fainted. To think that somebody would—"

"How about that?" Max asked. "Have you gotten a report from the doc yet?"

Halloran jerked a shoulder. "She had an inflamed appendix," he admitted grudgingly, "but that wasn't what killed her. She could have fainted, like you say, I suppose, but she was alive when the crazy bastard beat her and stuck his knife into her. The biting was *post mortem,* according to the doc, but—"

"Biting!" Sally gasped. "You mean he *bit* her?"

"Yeah." Halloran squeezed his lips together. "Sorry, Sally. I didn't intend to mention it. It's nothing to talk about. The guy who killed her was a sex-crazed fiend."

"How horrible!" She eyed him like a child waiting for words of wisdom from a respected elder. "Do you know who did it?"

"Not yet," Halloran admitted. He swung his eyes toward Max. "You said you saw seven or eight drops made. Did you peg any of them?"

"They looked like run-of-the-mill shoppers," Max told him. "Boosting is out of my territory. I haven't been keeping tabs on them. One of them was a good-looking blonde, though." He gave Sally a casual glance. "About Miss

Breeze's height and weight, maybe a little older. I think I'd recognize her if I saw her again. You want me to look through your picture gallery?"

Halloran grunted cynically.

Sally laughed, a trifle nervously Max thought, and said, "Gosh, listening to you two is giving me the willies! Don't you ever talk about anything besides crooks and murderers and dead bodies? I thought you were going to buy me some coffee, Zike."

"Sure, Sally. Got time?" Moving with surprising fluidity for a big man, Halloran got to his feet, then stood indecisively, staring at Max. "I ought to take you down for a statement and a look at the gallery, Keene."

"I don't feel like getting dressed and going out, Zike," Sally said. "How about getting a pot from one of the waiters? We can have our coffee here and you and Max can talk shop later."

"Well...okay." The plan obviously wasn't to Halloran's liking, but he hadn't much choice. "Want a sandwich, Sally?"

"Guess I may as well," she decided. "Make it a club on whole wheat. Want one, Max?"

"No, thanks," Max said, suppressing a grin. "Just coffee."

"Be right back," Halloran said gruffly. He strode out.

Max looked at the blonde and lifted an eyebrow. She returned the look with a frankness he hadn't expected and said, "He's nice—but a little dull. Thanks for not jerking the carpet out from under me."

"What time do you get through here?" Max asked in a low voice.

"My last act is at one."

"Suppose I tap on your door at around one-thirty?"

"All right." She nodded. "Know the address?"

"Yeah." He smiled slightly. "Leave the snake here."

She gave an amused giggle, like a small girl playing at sex, and said, "It's a girl snake, Max."

"How can you tell?" he asked.

Before she could reply, Halloran returned with a tray containing three cups of coffee and two sandwiches. He gave Max a swift, suspicious glance, as though he sensed a current of intrigue in the room, then he set a club sandwich and a cup of coffee beside Sally, put a ham-on-rye and a cup of coffee beside his own chair, and laid the tray on the trunk so Max could help himself to the remaining cup.

"Thanks," Max said.

"Don't mention it," Halloran replied gruffly. He sat down, and, in a tone which pointedly ignored Max, said to the blonde, "I talked to Joe Rawson this morning, Sally."

"Joe is okay." She bit a small corner off her sandwich, took a sip of coffee. Max noticed that her movements were delicate, precise, yet rhythmical. "How's he doing?"

"Going like a house afire," Halloran said it impressively, like a broker commenting on a bullish market. "He might be able to work you into the Glass Hat at the Congress."

"That's strictly a dance spot," she said, sounding uninterested.

"There's talk about a new management," Halloran went on. "If there's a change, Joe says The Modulators will get boosted into the number one music spot and they'll be looking for a socko act to feature in the ads. He thinks you might fit."

"Joe's full of hot air," she answered. "If he peddles anything to the Glass Hat, it'll be one of his own acts."

"You could sign with him," Halloran said gruffly. "Solly Franks is no damned good. Look how long you've been here. You ought to be getting a yard and a half a week, but Green's getting you for washers."

"Maybe I like the spot," Sally said lightly. "Thanks anyway, Zike. Elita wouldn't be happy in a noisy joint like the Glass Hat."

"Hell, the damned snake wouldn't know the difference," Halloran growled. "It's the dough that counts, isn't it? Once you're booked into a top spot like the Glass Hat, you'd have it made."

"Maybe," Sally said shortly. She finished half of the sandwich and pushed the rest away. "Want the rest of my sandwich, Max?"

"I'm figuring on a steak later," Max told her. "Thanks."

"Zike wants me to quit here and try for the big time," she went on, smiling at him over the edge of her coffee cup. "All cops think about is money. Are you that way, too, Max?"

Before Max could reply, Halloran growled, "Think about it, Sally. A yard and a half isn't chicken feed. Working in this joint is strictly for the birds. You ought to be up on top."

"I'll think about it, Zike." She set her coffee cup down and rose gracefully to her feet. "I'd better see how Elita is. It's nearly time for me to go on again." She managed a small wink at Max. "Gosh, I'll be glad when this night is over! I can't wait to hit the sack. Thanks for the coffee—and, Zike, drop in again soon, will you? You, too, Max." She moved lithely toward the door and went down the corridor.

Halloran was frowning like a man who'd discovered half a worm in an apple. Max looked at his watch. It was 9:45. He was in no hurry, but Halloran had to be written off and the sooner the cop was satisfied the easier things would be. If Halloran was soft for Sally Breeze, it might be smart to try for a quick break, while he was still under the spell.

"Well, how about it, sergeant?" Max said straight-faced. "Want me to go down and look at pictures?"

"That damn snake," Halloran muttered. "All she thinks about is that damn snake!" He looked up suddenly and stared at Max as though seeing him for the first time. "What'd you say, Keene?"

"I asked you if you wanted me to ride down and look through the gallery," Max said. "Tonight or tomorrow, it makes no difference to me." He grinned. "Unless you're figuring on hanging around to catch her act again."

"I'd better take you down now," Halloran decided. "I think your story is full of crap, but the lieutenant will want it in print. And it won't hurt for you to look through the gallery."

"Okay," Max said. "Let's roll."

"You know, if it isn't one damn thing, it's another..."

Max agreed, but he decided it might be wise to keep the opinion to himself. Sooner or later, Halloran might start wondering why Max had wandered into Sally Breeze's dressing room...

CHAPTER SIX

As SOON as he was out of the Tropic Isle and out from under Sally Breeze's spell, Sergeant Halloran became an efficient cog in the police machinery again and settled down to the business of questioning Max in detail about his afternoon's activities. Max repeated the story he had already related but, mainly to give himself some inner amusement, added a host of minute details of very little, if any, significance. Halloran grunted from time to time but seemed satisfied. At headquarters, Halloran commandeered a stenographer and made Max go over the whole thing again including, to Max's disgust, all the insignificant details. While the lengthy statement was being transcribed and typed, Halloran took Max to the B. of I. and supplied him with several huge piles of photos to scan. For the next two hours, Max shuffled desultorily through eight-by-ten glossies of male and female boosters from every big city in the nation.

Midway through, a name caught his eye: Walter Tom Friedl. He stopped, frowned, and tried to remember where he had heard the name. Then he remembered. Mabel Tangier had mentioned a Wally Friedl, a ghee who was bossing a string of girls locally. The photo showed a heavy-set man with short dark curly hair, large nose, square chin, a brooding expression in dark eyes.

According to the photostatted information, Friedl was 45 years old, weighed 195, and was five-eight in height. He came from Toledo, Ohio, and had a heist record a yard long, which was notable principally because of his few convictions. He'd lost twice—each time for an ace at Statesville—and currently was wanted for questioning about a fast shake that a department store in Milwaukee had suffered a year ago.

Max made a mental note of the details and continued through the piles of photos, giving special attention to females. There was nothing on Mabel Tangier, however, and none of the mugged babes resembled Sally Breeze in the least. His eyesight was beginning to blur when something about one of the pix made him go back for a double take. Vernon Wayne Price, age 28, weight 130, height five-nine, tapped in Waterloo, Iowa, for suspected shoplifting. He had beaten the rap, apparently, for no sentence was recorded. It was a poor picture, taken four years previously, but Vernon Wayne Price was undoubtedly Verne, the swish Max had seen at Mabel Tangier's apartment.

Feeling somewhat frustrated, Max went through the rest of the pix hurriedly, then returned to Homicide where Halloran was chewing a cigar and filling in blanks on a report form. The statement had been typed. Max glanced through it and scrawled a signature.

"Satisfied, sergeant?" Max stood up to go.

"How about the pictures?" Halloran asked.

"Blank," Max told him. "You know how lousy record shots are."

"Yeah." Halloran chewed the cigar viciously. "I don't know about this statement, Keene. To me, it smells. The lieutenant may want some more dope in the morning."

Max shrugged. "Tell him to call me. I've got an office, you know."

"Okay, beat it."

Max cabbed to Clark and Ohio, where he had ditched his Pontiac, and found an arrest ticket for overtime parking wired to the windshield wiper. Cussing mildly, he detached the ticket and crammed it into a pocket. He drove north slowly, toying with several ideas. Spotting a vacant space in front of the Embers on Dearborn Street, he remembered that he was hungry. He parked the Pontiac, went into the restaurant and ordered a roast beef dinner. When he finished eating, it was nearly one o'clock. He climbed into the Pontiac again and headed for Arlington Place.

There were no lights in Mabel Tangier's apartment; in fact, the entire building was dark. Max parked in front of it, turned off the ignition, and lit a cigarette. The street was shadowy and quiet. Max relaxed and concentrated on the general situation. For the moment, Halloran was satisfied. But there were holes in the statement—from the viewpoint of a cop, at any rate. Also, Halloran would start wondering what Max had wanted with Sally Breeze. Unless he was damned careful, he was liable to find himself jammed up tight.

Almost exactly on the stroke of one-thirty, headlights sliced into Arlington Place and a dark sedan screeched to a stop in front of Sally Breeze's building. She got out, the blue dress tight across her rounded hips, holding the hat box in one hand, and he heard her husky contralto call, "Thanks a lot, Buck!" A deep male voice replied, "Call me in the morning, Sal."

The general darkness plus the glare of the headlights made it impossible for Max to spot the driver of the car through its windshield, but its front license plate was visible. Automatically, Max made a mental note of the number—Illinois 333-876—an easy combination to remember. As the sedan's door slammed and Sally ran toward the entrance of her building, Max noticed a detail that made his eyebrows lift with surprise: A slender rod antenna rose from a heavy insulator fixed to the sedan's rear fender, indicating a two-way radio, probably located in the car's trunk. That meant a cop or a cabbie—and the sedan sure as hell wasn't a taxi. A couple of richards had piloted Sally Breeze home after her last hot stint with the coiling snake, Max deduced. And she was on intimate, friendly terms with them, too...

Max gave her five minutes, then got out of the Pontiac and crossed the street. The door release responded to his ring immediately and, humming tonelessly, he mounted two flights of carpeted stairs to the third floor. A door stood open. Smiling thinly, he drummed his knuckles against the jamb and walked in. From an inner room, her husky voice called, "Be right with you, Max. Make yourself at home."

It was a comfortable living room, a cross between Grand Rapids Practical and Michigan Avenue Moderne. The chairs and couch were large, solid, and plastic-veneered in a shiny grayish grain. Tufty, pastel-colored upholstery and matching floor-length drapes. A couple of good Dufy prints on the wall. Most of the stuff was her own, he surmised. Some of it was expensive. It looked like a living room, bedroom, dinette set-up. A yard and a half a month, easily, he figured.

A fake alligator-grain violin case stood in a corner beside a magazine-jammed bookcase. Max eyed it skeptically, then noticed the chrome music stand near the windows. He walked toward it and stared at the heavily note-dotted page of a Beethoven concerto. The music meant nothing to him, but he was impressed. Beethoven was long hair and if she could handle the violin as well as she did the snake there was more to her than he had thought.

"Like music, Max?" She had returned silently, and, when he turned, he saw that she had changed into a dark satin robe that fitted her loosely but effectively.

"Sure," he said agreeably. "I didn't know you fiddled."

"I'm not very good." She smiled. "Elita likes Beethoven. I don't know why."

"Elita's the snake?"

"Yes. Whenever she gets temperamental, I give her a dose of Beethoven and she gets sweet and docile again." She laughed softly. "You don't like Elita. You're wrinkling your nose."

"I can think of better playmates," he admitted.

"So can I." She winked in a way that left very little doubt as to her meaning, and asked, "How about a drink?"

"Whatever you're having."

"Scotch it is, then. Soda or branch water?"

"A little soda."

She glided toward a combination dinette and kitchen. Max followed her and watched silently while she splashed generous quantities of Highland Queen into glasses and opened a fresh bottle of soda. She sprinkled a little of the soda into each of the glasses, handed him one, and preceded him back to the living room. She sat down on the big couch and patted the cushion beside her.

"Sit here, Max. It's cozier." She smiled as she lifted her glass. "Cheers."

Max sat beside her and said, "Cheers." He took a large swallow. It was good liquor.

"I suppose you want to get down to business," she said in a half-teasing, half-mocking tone.

"Might as well," he agreed.

"Well—" She frowned slightly and pursed her red lips. "I honestly don't know where to begin, Max. If you were there, you saw what happened. I went in with the packages, left them on the table, and walked out. I didn't know who was going to pick them up. I didn't even wonder about it. And I hardly gave the cashier a glance."

"What was in the packages?" Max asked.

"I don't know."

"Hell, you lifted them, didn't you?"

"No." She shook her head, and, seeing the cynical expression in his eyes, added, "Honest, Max, I never stole anything in my life."

"Where'd you get them, then?"

"I was told to go to the lingerie counter on the first floor of Shield's at exactly 12:45 and ask for a pale blue strapless bra, size 36. There was a thin-faced, rather elderly man behind the counter, and, when I told him what I wanted, he got the packages out, showed me some bras, and made out a sales slip for $3.57. I paid him, picked up the packages, and went straight to the cafeteria."

"Wait a minute. *Who* told you to go to Shield's?"

"I don't know that either, Max. I got a phone call, telling me to follow instructions—or else."

"Or else what?"

"I could go back to Indianapolis and hustle dishes for a living."

"For cryin' out loud, you must think I'm a stupe." Max lifted his glass and swallowed a double gulp of the mellow liquor.

"You don't believe me?"

"Look, Sally." He lowered the glass and faced her. "I've been private dicking a long time. I caught your act and I talked to Danny Green. He told me you were solid. In other words, the customers like you and you're making dough for the joint. So he's not going to kick you out, even if the cops hang a petty larceny tag on you. As far as I'm concerned, you can forget a build-up. If you're a klepto, just say so. Lots of dames are. It's a sort of disease and I don't give a damn about it one way or another. What I want to know is who's behind the racket and who had a string on the kid who got killed. I'm not going to holler cop, either. It's personal, understand? They suckered me and I don't like it."

"You sound like a right guy, Max. How can I make you believe me?"

"You might try telling me the truth."

She was silent a moment, then she sighed softly and rested her head against the back of the couch. The position accentuated the full curve of her breasts. Max eyed them appreciatively and decided that calling her a girl was like calling a Cadillac a car.

"All right," she said. She swished the liquor around in her glass, then drained it. She dropped the empty glass to the floor. "It's not easy to talk about, Max. Maybe you'll understand. I hope so. I've been needing to talk to someone about it, and it may as well be you. Maybe it'll help you, maybe it won't. If it doesn't, I'm trusting you to forget the whole thing. Okay?"

"I'm not gassy," Max said.

"I figured that. Well, it all started a long time ago, I suppose. Back when I was in high school. Indianapolis. My mother was a music teacher. My father ran a hardware store. I began studying piano when I was a little kid, then switched to the violin and got pretty good. Dad played the viola and we used to do some nice trios in the evenings. But it sort of got me off the beam. As a kid, I mean. There was always a lot of practicing to do and I never got to run around like the other kids did. Things were different when I got to high school, though. I met some boys who had cars—and there were a lot of parties going on—and, well, I started to let the violin get kind of dusty. To make a long story short, I worked as a waitress for a while after graduation and met a guy from New York. He had a line that was strictly muck, but I swallowed it, only to discover a month later what happens to girls who go to motels with traveling salesmen. I was scared silly, more because of how it would affect my parents than for what might happen to me. So I quit my job, packed a suitcase, and headed for Chicago." She contemplated a red fingernail. "That was three years ago."

"Tough," Max commented.

"You don't know the half of it. I lived in a west side rooming house and wagged my tail up and down a counter for five months, trying to save every nickel I could. It was a hell of a waste. The kid was born dead and by the time I was on my feet again, I looked a wreck and hardly had a decent dress to my name. I got a job serving drinks in a northside spot. I started saving dough again—and I kept my eyes open. One night one of the fiddlers didn't show up and just for laughs I picked up his instrument and gave the customers some Blue Danube. It went over big and I started thinking about getting into show biz. I talked to some of the girls whenever I got a chance and they wised me up. I built up a wardrobe, bought a fiddle, had a photographer make some publicity shots, and started looking for an agent. I had myself figured as a gypsy-type fiddler, the kind some of the swank spots feature as an inducement to light amour and heavy drinking. If you know anything about the racket, you probably know what happened."

"No soap," Max guessed.

"Right." She grimaced wryly. "The agents took one look at me and turned thumbs down. Wrong type. No girl could be a gypsy violinist unless she was thin as a rail, talked broken English, and had stringy black hair. I was the sexy type, it seems, and as far as they were concerned I could drop dead or come back when I had an act they could peddle."

"Who'd you contact?"

"All of them. They all gave me the same line. So I bought a G-string and some ballet lessons. One of my ballet teachers suggested the snake. Said it would give the act class and draw attention. I was willing to try anything at that point, so I saved up enough dough to buy Elita. She drew attention, all right, and Solly Franks agreed to take me on, but I was still poison to the joints. Solly tried to get me in here and there, but it was no dice."

"Why?" Max asked.

"No reason. I was about to give Elita to some zoo and go back to slinging hash when I got the first telephone call." She paused. "How about another drink?"

"I'll get them." Max collected the glasses, went to the kitchen, refilled them. When he returned, she had rearranged the cushions on the couch and was stretched upon it, her eyes closed and her long sleek legs peeking from the fold of the robe. He touched her hand with the glass. She opened her eyes, smiled, and made room for him beside her. He sat down, conscious of the pressure of her hip against his.

"You were telling me about the first call," Max reminded her.

"I had a room on LaSalle Street at the time," she told him. "As I said, I was about to give up. I was sitting there, playing with Elita and wondering if I'd been jinxed some way, when the landlady knocked on the door and said I was wanted on the phone. It was a man's voice, one I didn't recognize. He asked if I wanted a club date. Naturally, I said yes. He told me to go to Larsen's jewelry department the next afternoon at exactly one o'clock and to ask to see some cocktail rings. The clerk would put some packages on the counter near me, he said, and I was to take them to a certain restaurant and leave them on a table. At first I thought it was a gag. But I was desperate enough to try anything, so I wandered down to Larsen's the next day and tried on some rings. The clerk produced the packages and I delivered them to the restaurant. When I got back to my room, the phone was ringing and it was Solly Franks. He said the Tropic Isle had an opening for me." She shrugged. "Believe it or not."

"How long ago was that?"

"About nine months ago, I guess."

"You still don't know who calls?"

"No. It's always the same voice, and I've talked to him two or three times a week for months now, but I haven't the slightest idea who it is. All I know is that I've got a job and a fairly decent apartment and can do pretty much as I please as long as I follow instructions." She drank from her glass, then added, "That's why I soft-pedaled Zike's offer to get me in at the Glass Hat. Maybe Zike's connection is good, but I know I'm not a great *artiste*—and I'm damned leery of the good intentions of agents. Besides, mystery voice might get the idea that I was stepping out of line, and I'm not anxious to waltz entrees for a living again. You don't blame me, do you, Max?" There was a plaintive note in her voice.

"I don't know." It was a plain statement of fact. The story was screwy, but she sounded sincere. Max knew enough about the entertainment racket to know that it was full of angles, and he knew that a young girl alone in a big city could easily be tempted. Hell, a lot of girls had had to do more than transport hot merchandise for a chance in the spotlight. In a way, it had been a break; if he had been in her shoes, he'd have taken it, too.

"You believe me, don't you?"

"Sure, kid."

She set her glass on the floor, lifted her arms, and slid her hands around his neck. "You're a nice guy, Max. I'm glad I told you," she whispered. "I feel good now. Better than I've felt in years. I've been needing someone like you."

Her arms were tugging at him and her eyes were warm pits of primitive desire. He lowered his glass to the floor and leaned down. She pulled her body against his. It was a long kiss, meant to arouse him—and it did. He unfastened her robe, parted it, and heard her sigh. There was nothing beneath the robe, just a smooth, voluptuous, eager body.

"Turn off the light, darling..." she whispered.

CHAPTER SEVEN

HE DISENTANGLED himself from her embrace and sat up. His foot nudged the glass he had set on the floor, and, bending cautiously, he felt around in the darkness, located it, raised it to his lips. The couch creaked, and, murmuring drowsily, she asked, "Max...?"

"Uh-huh."

"What are you doing?"

"Leaving."

"But...the night's young..."

"Yeah, but I'm not."

He felt her move restlessly and sensed that her eyes were probing the darkness. He sat down, took her in his arms, and kissed her. She wound her arms around him, holding him so tightly that, had he been twenty pounds lighter, part of her would have gone right through him. The kiss lasted longer than he had planned, but he freed himself eventually and mumbled good night.

"Call me?" she whispered.

"Sure," he promised.

"When?"

"Soon."

He thrust his arms into his jacket and groped his way to the door. He had found the latch and was releasing it when she called softly, "Be careful, darling..." He mumbled a syllable of reassurance, opened the door, stepped into the dimly lighted corridor. He stood there a moment, waiting for the click of the latch, then went quietly downstairs. Outside, the street was silent and dark and the stagnant night air was as warm and sticky as a young man's dream. It was 3:29.

He had paused in the doorway, about to step to the sidewalk and cross the street toward his car, when the first shot rang out. He saw a yellowish streak of fire coming from a sedan parked down the street, felt the smash of the lead as it drilled into the side of the doorway, then he heard the bang. The second shot caught his arm and flung it violently around. Instinctively, he spun with the blow and crumpled to the sidewalk, clawing for his gun, but it was pinned under his body.

He could only curse fervently and forced himself to lie still. A car's engine roared and he felt rather than saw the sedan as it rolled past him. A third bullet chipped cement onto his face, then ricocheted into the door, shattering the glass. Then the car was gone.

Max got slowly to his feet, clasping his left arm, which felt strangely numb. Windows were being raised and people were craning out, staring toward him. Someone shouted. From a distance, a siren began to wail. Max cursed and tried to move his arm. The numbness was fading and pain was shooting toward his shoulder. The bastards had winged him. But he'd been lucky. Damned lucky.

A squad car careened around the corner, its siren screaming like a cat in heat. Its headlights floodlighted him against the building. "What the hell's going on?" a harsh voice demanded. Two cops jumped out and strode toward him.

From a window above, a female voice screeched, "They tried to kill him! They shot three times!"

"You okay?" the younger of the two cops demanded.

"Yeah." Max gritted his teeth. "They got me in the arm, that's all."

"You spot them?"

Max hesitated, then rasped, "Yeah. It was a sedan, a dark blue or black sedan with—" He groaned and let them have a glimpse of his blood-soaked fingers. "I need a doc—"

The other cop had been peering at him. "I've seen you around somewhere. What's your name?"

"Max Keene. I'm a private dick." He groaned again. "For God's sake, boys, get me to a doc, will you?"

"Hell, yes. St. Joseph's is the nearest hospital. We'll take you there. Did you peg the license?"

Max groaned, closed his eyes, and swayed realistically. The arm wasn't hurting that much, but he wanted time to add things together. "Hell," he muttered in agonized tones, "can't we talk about this later?"

"Well...okay."

They helped him into the back of the squad car and took him to the emergency room at St. Joseph's. The bullet had torn through the fleshy part of a muscle and grazed the bone. It would be painful for several weeks, the doctor surmised, but barring infection, would heal without impairing the arm. While the wound was being cleansed and bandaged, Max squeezed his eyes shut and thought about Sally Breeze and the dark sedan. He could be wrong, of course, but whoever had lain in wait for him had known that he was in the blonde's apartment. Sally could have mentioned their date. Hell, she *must* have mentioned it. It didn't add any other way. So the dark sedan...

"All right, Mr. Keene," the doctor said briskly. "Take it easy, now. Come in tomorrow afternoon and I'll check the dressing."

"Thanks, doc." Max got to his feet and walked out to where the two cops were waiting. "Looks like I'm going to live," he told them. "I suppose you want a statement."

"Well, we got to make a report, Keene." The younger cop grinned and got out a notebook. "Sometimes it's easier when a guy gets killed. Not so much paperwork, you know."

"Yeah." Max nodded and stared at the cop's notebook.

It was a shiny new notebook, and, judging by the way the young cop was wriggling his pencil, he was itching to dash off a report that would singe the captain's eyebrows. Max had other ideas. "Well, here's what happened:

I've got a client, a rich guy with a good-looking young wife, who thinks maybe she's been stepping out on him. You know how it goes. Anyway, he's out of town and hired me to keep an eye on her. I picked her up about two a.m. outside the Ambassador West and tailed her cab to the corner of Clark and Diversey. She walked east on Diversey and went into a joint there and didn't come out until 3:30. Probably lapping it up. I got on her tail again and followed her south on Clark to Arlington Place. She ducked into one of the buildings along there. I figured she had spotted me and was trying to give me the slip, so I cruised on past, came back, and parked. I was checking the doorways, trying to figure out where she'd gone, when a sedan came east on Arlington, slowed down beside me, and began spitting lead. A slug hit me in the arm. As I fell, I grabbed a quick look at the car's plates. They were Illinois plates, number 333-876. Whoever was in the car fired three shots, then scrammed."

"Hell, that's not much of a statement." The cop scowled at his notebook. "Who's this client?"

"I can't give you his name, for obvious reasons."

"But maybe her boyfriend did the shooting."

"Could be." Max shrugged.

"But—"

"Look," Max snapped. "I'm the guy who got gunned—not you. All you got to do is write that down and throw it in the box at headquarters. If the captain's got questions, he knows where to find me. I'll tell him exactly what I told you. In the meantime, you've got those plate numbers. Get them checked. When you locate the owner of that sedan, I'll sign a complaint. In the meantime, I'm going to call it a night. How about driving me around to where my car is parked?"

"But all you've said is that—"

"It's no skin off us," the older cop interrupted, yawning. "Like he says, he's the guy who got shot. Let's knock it off."

"But—" The younger cop was still scowling.

"Come on, Joe, no use knocking yourself out." His partner yawned again and started toward the squad car. "We'll drop him off and then grab ourselves some coffee. No one's going to blame you if a private dick gets himself shot at."

The younger cop grumbled like a second-class Boy Scout who hated to see a bowline fumbled, but he climbed into the squad car and piloted it back to Arlington Place. The Pontiac was where Max had left it. He got in, waved to the cops, and worked his car into the street. It was awkward driving with one hand, but fortunately there was very little traffic. He reached Elm Street, maneuvered the Pontiac into a parking spot, and walked wearily into the apartment hotel he called home. Without bothering to undress, he dropped onto his bed and closed his eyes. He tossed restlessly for several minutes, then began to snore...

A steady pounding awakened him. He started to roll over, winced, and remembered his wounded arm. He sat up gingerly and shouted, "Wait a minute, can't you?" The pounding stopped and an impatient voice, filtered through the wooden door, rasped, "Thought you were dead. Open up." Max glanced at his watch. It was 8:21, an hour no friend would choose for visiting. Tightening his lips slightly, he got up, walked to his dresser, took out his .38. Then he opened the door.

The man in the corridor was big, red-faced, well dressed and had COP written all over him. His nostrils dilated slightly at sight of the gun in Max's hand, but his eyes remained flat and opaque, as though charged with a hidden anger. He moved into the small apartment brusquely, saying, "Put away that rod, Keene. I'm Sergeant Nehlson. Police." Max noticed that he walked with a bowlegged step, as though he were wearing wet drawers.

"What's up?" Max asked. He went back to the bed and sat down, keeping the gun beside him.

The big cop stared around the room, went to the window, glanced out. Then he picked out a chair near Max and sat down, being careful not to abuse the crease in his lightweight flannel slacks. "I hear you got gunned last night," he commented heavily. His eyes plucked at the bloodstained shirt Max still wore.

"Yeah," Max said wearily. He could recall no Sergeant Nehlson being attached to the district station, a fact that bothered him. Nehlson could be a richard from downtown, of course—but he could also be an ex-cop, one who had decided not to work for peanuts. His attitude and clothes suggested the latter—and there was a telltale bulge that betrayed the presence of a gun beneath the well-draped jacket. "So what?" Max asked.

"Tell me about it."

"I made a statement last night."

"I read it," Nehlson chuckled. "You were pretty mixed up."

"In what way?"

"Well, according to your statement, you were wandering down Arlington Place, peeking in doorways, and a dark sedan came along and blasted you. The gunman scored one hit and two misses. While you were under fire, you fell to the sidewalk but managed to get a look at the car's plates. They were Illinois plates, number 333-876." Nehlson smiled and paused like a man who obviously loved good things—liquor, clothes, food—but none as much as the sound of his own voice. "Am I right, Keene?"

"Yeah."

"Well, it's a lot of crap."

"Why?"

Nehlson's smile vanished as though jerked away by an invisible string and a hard look narrowed his eyes. "Because *I* drive a dark blue sedan—and *my* plates are number 333-876. How do you like *them* apples, shamus?"

Max jiggled an eyebrow. "That's interesting," he said casually. "Who was driving it at about 3:30 this a.m.?"

"Nobody!" Nehlson's voice was as flat as a bride's first cake—and as dangerous. "It was parked outside the Melody Bar on Clark from 3:20 to 4:15."

"You're sure?"

"I'm damn sure. You made a mistake, shamus, a mistake that could be damned embarrassing to me." Nehlson stripped cellophane from a cigar and tore a match from a packet with a violent gesture. "Am I right?"

Max rolled a lip. "I know what I saw," he said quietly.

"Keene, don't be a damn fool!" Nehlson said vehemently. He exhaled a cloud of Havana-scented smoke and folded his arms across his chest as though trying to keep his rib cage from exploding with anger. "Let me spell it out for you. My car was locked. It was parked in front of the Melody Bar. I was inside the place, checking on a couple of dames. The bartender could see my car through the windows and the dames will remember the cop who gave them some good advice. You haven't got a chance of convincing anybody it was my car you saw, so why not admit the whole thing was a mistake? Go down and change your statement. You were excited. You got the numbers twisted, maybe. Anybody can understand a mistake like that. Catch on?"

"Sure." Max forced a smile. "Except one thing."

"What's that?"

"If you've got such an airtight alibi, what are you so worried about?"

"Not a damn thing." Nehlson poked the end of the cigar at Max as though he was taking aim with a dart. "I've got a good record. And I can take care of myself, Keene. You're the guy I'm worried about. You're supposed to be a smart private dick, but you're acting like a guy with a lot of screws loose. That statement of yours was strictly for the birds. Maybe you were doing a tail job, but I got a hunch it wasn't the kind of tail you said. That's okay with me, though; I go for that stuff myself." He winked broadly. "But because the babe's husband got wise and took a shot at you, that doesn't entitle you to set me up for a lot of wisecracks from the other cops and put me in a spot where some stupe from one of the newspapers could try to make something of it. Get my point? For a guy who can't have too many friends at headquarters, you've come damned close to making a bad stink right where you live. Luckily, one of the boys spotted it and tipped me, and you can fix the mistake without much trouble to either of us. See what I mean?"

"Sure, sergeant."

"Okay." Nehlson stood up and smiled expansively. "Go down and fix it right away, Keene. The sooner the better for all concerned." He rose leisurely, and as though suddenly remembering something, unclamped the cigar from his teeth and pointed it at Max's arm. "Looks like you got winged."

"Yeah."

"Nothing broken?"

"No."

"Well, better take it easy. It could get infected, you know." Nelhson turned and walked out the door, closing it behind him.

Max stared at the closed door for a long moment, then muttered a deeply felt comment. Max stripped off his clothes, bathed, shaved, and got into clean underclothes. He was searching for a shirt when he noticed the time. He went to the phone and called Jim Barone.

"Jim? Max."

"Well, are you in or out?" Barone asked.

"Out." Max grinned. "You can skip the writ."

"What happened?"

"Let's talk about it later. Right now I've got a few questions."

"Well, hurry up. I have to file an appearance."

"Who was the Parreo kid divorcing?"

"A no-good husband named Jason Clements. He ditched her for another babe and went west. Why?"

"He's not in Chicago, then?"

"Not to my knowledge."

"Okay. Ever hear of a cop sergeant named Nehlson?"

"Buck Nehlson? Sure. He's attached to Vice."

"Who does he work with?"

"A sharpie named Donigan. Ray Donigan. Big square-faced kid."

"Thanks, Jim. See you at the office."

"You bet."

Max hung up, thumbed through the directory, and found Gwen Collyer's number. There was a warm sleepiness in her voice when she answered and Max imagined her curved across tousled sheets and bending like September Morn over the phone. It was a pretty picture. The red hair gave it a nice touch.

"This is Max Keene, kiddo," he said. "You still looking for a job?"

"What would I do with a job? I've nearly learned to live without one." The sleepiness faded from her voice. She sounded eager. "Did you locate something for me, Max? No kidding?"

"Put on your face and go over to Little Harry's Lounge." He gave her the address. "I gave you a build-up and he's willing to take a chance. It's not a classy joint, but the dough he pays is negotiable and it'll be a start. He's expecting you some time this morning."

"Wonderful! Who do I ask for?"

"Little Harry. He's a big fat slob but okay. Let him look but not touch. Understand?"

"Lips that touch liquor shall never touch mine, huh? Do I ask for a salary—or is this educational?"

"Harry's square. Take whatever he offers. If you click at all, he'll pass the word to Solly Franks, the agent, and you'll be booked regularly. Just give with the hips and the lips, kiddo, and make the customers think you're enjoying it. I'll try to look in on you tonight."

"Max—" There was a moment of silence, as though she were searching for words, then, "Max, I'm real grateful."

"Forget it, kiddo," he said gruffly. "See you tonight."

CHAPTER EIGHT

AFTER WANDERING through a drapery department, a book department, and a rug section, Max located the third floor office of Shield's chief store detective. The sign on the door read: *SPECIAL SERVICES, Mr. Thomas Ames.* In the outer office, two bulky women were putting the petty theft strong arm to a smaller woman who, through freely flowing tears, was protesting that she didn't know why she did it. Max worked his way around them and went to an inner door marked *Private.* He knocked tentatively, then turned the knob. Tom Ames looked up, started to glare, then said, "Max—how the hell are you?"

"Pretty good." Max closed the door. "Busy?"

"Like a boarding-house john," Ames said. He tossed his pen to the desk. "Hell, sit down, Max. It must be a couple of years since I saw you. You still private dicking?"

"Sure. Looks like you fell into gravy, Tom."

"It's a good job," Ames admitted. "They keep me damned busy, though. If you're looking for some fast dope on one of our customers, I'm afraid you're out of luck, Max. I've had a constant procession through here all morning, and—"

"They hitting you pretty hard?"

Ames deliberated a moment. His face was round and red and damp, resembling a boiled beet, but the job at Shield's, Max noted, had given him an executive air. Ames had been a city cop, had switched to private dicking, and then, finding the going too rough for a family man, had slipped into the Special Services berth at the big store. "There's no denying it," Ames said slowly. "Our inventory loss has been jumping like crazy. I've got a large crew of experienced operatives spotted throughout the store, and they're onto every dodge that's ever been worked. But all they've been pulling in are society kleptos and senile housewives who think that getting away with a bathroom mop is a big deal." Ames shrugged. "Hell, Max, you didn't come here to listen to my troubles. You married yet?"

"Why should I get married?" Max grinned. "She isn't even pregnant."

Ames laughed. "I thought you might want to dicker for a discount on a bridal outfit."

"As a matter of fact," Max told him, "I'm interested in your troubles, Tom. Don't get me wrong, I'm not looking for a job. But I've stumbled on a few things in the last couple of days that make me think that boosting has gotten organized recently."

"Organized?" Ames looked dubious. "Hell, the racket's always been small-time. It's a one or two-man operation— and once they're spotted they're out of business. The next time they come in the door, we give them the quick goodbye. It's these screwball kleptos that drive us nuts. They'll glom onto anything that isn't bolted down, and—"

"You're off, Tom, way off," Max interrupted. "There's an organized gang looting the store, probably with the connivance of some of your most trusted employees. I can't prove it, but I can give you a fairly accurate picture of the M.O."

"I'm listening."

Max sketched in detail the manner in which Sally Breeze had approached the lingerie counter and walked away with two packages, then he added several touches from what Little Harry had told him about the modernized business methods of the fence racket. "In other words, as I see it, Tom," he concluded, "it isn't haphazard boosting. It's organized theft, with an inside man doing the fingering. The actual pass is accomplished by an outsider who simply carries the loot past the doors and takes it on to a drop. They probably know precisely what they want and switch their activity from department to department, depending on what kind of orders they have on file."

"If it isn't one damned thing it's another," Ames said with feeling. "I can't stop and search everybody who leaves the store!"

"Can you work from the emplcyee end?"

"Sure—but hell, do you know how many clerks, buyers, cashiers, wrappers, floormen and minor executives this size store has?"

"Plenty, I suppose. But that's your problem. Yesterday at 12:45 a pick-up girl went to the lingerie department on the first floor and asked to see a pale blue strapless bra She was waited on by a thin-faced, rather elderly man who made out a $3.57 sales check for the bra and put two fairly large-sized boxes within her reach. She walked out with the boxes. I saw the drop but lost the trail. Car you check yesterday's sales and find out which clerk was on duty?"

"Sure." Ames scowled. "That part's easy. But the chances are that the regular clerk went off to lunch—in fact, I'm damned sure of it, because the clerks in lingerie are all women—so one of the floormen must have taken over. And when he wrote up the sale he probably used one of the regular clerk's books. She wouldn't think anything of it, because the girls get a commission on sales—and the floormen don't. Even if I asked her about it, she probably wouldn't admit it."

"What's in the lingerie department that's worth stealing?" Max asked.

"Are you kidding? We've got some little imported lace numbers that sell for a couple of hundred bucks a copy!

Three or four of those in a small box and—*whew!*" Ames looked ill. "How long do you think this has been going on?"

"Eight or nine months, at least. Maybe longer."

"What's your angle, Max?"

"I'd like to know who's fagin-ing the deal." Max unbuttoned his jacket and gave Ames a glimpse of his bandaged arm. "I got a slug in the arm last night—and a young kid got knifed yesterday afternoon. I think it ties into the racket."

"Have you talked to any of the other stores?"

"Not yet."

"Well, if they've started shooting, it's because they're uneasy. They must feel that you're crowding them." Ames scowled at his desk. "They've already killed a kid, you say. That means it's a big operation. They wouldn't be taking a chance with The Baker, otherwise."

"It's big, all right," Max assured him. "Add it up."

"Right now I'm confused, Max," Ames admitted. "Let me think about this for a while. I don't want to go off half-cocked—and I don't want to miss any bets, either. Suppose I spot the guy who made the pass. What do you want me to do?"

"Hang a couple of good eyes on him. Check his employment record. Get a set of his prints. Then give him a chance to hang himself," Max said. "I'd like a breakdown of what develops, of course."

Ames nodded. "Okay, I'll go to work on it right away. Where can I reach you?"

"My office phone is in the book. If I'm not in, leave your number. I'll check regularly with the answering service and call you back."

"Fine." Ames shook his head. "You've given me a big headache, Max—but don't think I'm not grateful. If I can wangle you a fee—"

"Forget it, Tom," Max said, rising. "This is on the cuff. Just keep an eye on the candy and don't let them scent a tip-off. I've a personal interest in the bossman."

For the next two hours, Max toured the Special Services offices of the big Loop stores, accumulating a variety of reactions. Several were frankly incredulous, but all were more than a little interested. Larsen's admitted a high rate of loss in their fur and accessories departments. Steven's had been hit badly in their custom footwear and bridal shops. The Hub had noticed an inexplicable disappearance of cashmere sweaters and coats. All promised to tighten their security precautions and to keep watch for the type of passing operation that Max described. Max was riding the escalator in The Fair store when he sensed that he was being followed.

He glanced casually around. Behind him on the moving stairs was a straggly line of ordinary-looking people. Two young and giggling schoolgirls. A frowning, kerchief-wearing woman with a shopping bag. A clerkish, gray-haired man. A tightly corseted woman carrying a briefcase. Another woman, older, arms laden with packages. He catalogued them automatically, stepped off at the fifth floor, and strolled slowly to the elevators. When an UP car came along, he got on and rode to Eight. He stepped out, and, seeing the store's cafeteria, remembered that he hadn't eaten lunch. He got into line, pushing his tray along the polished rails choosily, and helped himself to a chicken potpie, a hard roll, a slice of blueberry pie, and a cup of coffee. When he reached the cashier, he glanced down the line. Kerchief, Gray Hair and Corset were behind him. Max parted with $1.15 and carried his tray to a table close to the exit.

He ate with deliberate slowness, waiting to see what, if anything, happened. Kerchief devoured a hot beef sandwich, drank a glass of milk, and hurried out with her shopping bag. Corset fiddled around with a sparse helping of Spanish rice and sipped a cup of coffee nervously while leafing through a sheaf of papers that she had taken from the briefcase. Gray Hair chewed thoughtfully at a slice of chocolate cake. Max began on the blueberry pie. Gray Hair took out a notebook and a pencil and began making detailed notes about something. Corset stuffed the papers into her briefcase, glanced at her watch, and began fiddling with a lipstick and mirror. Max lit a cigarette. Corset gathered her things together and bustled out. Max sighed and glanced somberly at Gray Hair. The clerkish guy was staring at his notes, as though attempting to memorize them. Max grinned inwardly, drank his coffee, and rose abruptly. He strode toward the exit.

When he reached State Street, Max slowed his pace and walked leisurely to the parking lot where he had left his car. He drove slowly and cautiously, paying no attention to the cars behind him, until he reached Chicago Avenue. He went west to Clark, parked, and headed for his office. The phone was ringing when he opened the door. Ignoring it, he went to the window and peeked out. Gray Hair was climbing out of a yellow Chevy sedan. Max grunted and picked up the phone.

"Hello?" he said tonelessly.

"Keene?" a deep voice demanded. "This is Nehlson, Sergeant Nehlson. Where the hell have you been?" Nehlson sounded as though somebody had been kneading his guts.

"On a job," Max told him. "Why?"

"You didn't correct your statement yet."

"Hell, that's right."

"Come right down and take care of it. Understand?"

"Guess I'd better. Thanks for reminding me, sergeant."

Max stared at the wall.

"I'm not kidding, Keene," Nehlson warned. "You're putting me on the spot, dammit!"

"It slipped my mind. Don't worry about it."

"You'll come right down?"

"Sure thing, sergeant. Relax."

The phone banged in Max's ear, betraying the violence of Sergeant Nehlson's mood. Max checked with the answering service, then looked up Sally Breeze's number. The receiver played an electronic staccato in his ear but no one answered. Max frowned, went to the window again, peered out. Gray Hair was standing across the street, in front of the corner drugstore, studying a racing form. Max studied him critically, then shook his head and went next door to see Jim Barone.

The lawyer was typing a detailed description of some tavern fixtures into a Cole bill-of-sale form. He looked up as Max entered and said, "Well, finally. What's going on?"

Max told him.

Jim Barone pursed his lips and frowned. "You're a sucker to tangle with them," he advised. "The take must run to big dough—and they've obviously gone to a lot of trouble to set it up. Whoever's running things won't hold still for interference from you. Keep poking your nose into things and you'll have the life expectancy of a match."

"I've got an angle," Max commented.

"Helen Parreo?" Barone passed an impatient hand over his thinning hair. "She was a nice kid and she got killed. Okay, murder's a crime—it's a job for the cops, not you. I represented her. I lost a fee because she got killed. Am I going to chase out and try to stir up a lot of—"

"I said I had an angle," Max repeated.

"The stores?" Barone snorted. "Don't be a sap, Max. The State Street Association might send you a letter of thanks—but that's all. When it comes to dough, they're tighter than Aunt Nelly. If you're looking for a case with possibilities, I've got an action in court that might—"

"You missed the point, Jim," Max interrupted. "I'm not looking for dough, not right now. I'm thinking about all these kids that the racket has sucked in."

"What about them?"

"Don't they deserve a chance?"

"Sure, but—" Barone shrugged.

"They're not getting it, Jim."

Barone was silent a while. "Okay, Max," he said at last. "I think you're a damn fool, but I'll keep a *habeas* writ handy. Let me know if there's anything I can do."

"Thanks, Jim. I'll check with you in the morning."

When Max returned to his office, Gray Hair was still on the corner, looking a little bored with the racing form. Max tried Sally Breeze's number again. Still no answer. It wasn't quite five o'clock, too early for her to have gone to the Tropic Isle. Max smoked a cigarette and thought about Sergeant Nehlson. Nehlson sure as hell was anxious not to be tied to the shooting...

With a curious smile on his lips, Max pulled the phone toward him and dialed the *Tribune*. When a pleasant feminine voice answered, he asked for the City Room. The pleasant voice went away and a hurried male one took its place. Max asked if Abe Simon was around. There was a long wait, during which he listened to a babble of voices and the clicking of machines, then Abe Simon's voice said, "This is Simon."

"Abe, this is an anonymous call," Max said carefully. "Understand?"

"With that washboard tenor of yours?" Abe's laugh rattled the receiver. "So you're anonymous. Who's sleeping with whom, I hope, huh?"

"There was a shooting early this morning on Arlington Place. A private dick named Max Keene was fired upon from a dark blue sedan. Three shots were fired and Keene stopped one with an arm. He fell to the sidewalk but he managed to peg the license of the car. The sedan carried Illinois plates #333-876. A squad car rushed Keene to the emergency room at St. Joseph's Hospital, and after treatment Keene made a statement to the district police, identifying the sedan. Got it?"

The wire hummed a while. "Well, I don't know...who belongs to the sedan?"

"A police sergeant assigned to Vice, named Buck Nehlson."

"The hell you say. They're keeping it quiet, huh?"

"Looks like it."

"Swell. The Colonel loves this kind of stuff. I'll item it pronto."

"Thanks much, Abe."

"Thank *you*, shamus."

Max sat at his desk for several minutes, cautiously flexing his wounded arm. Pain stabbed toward his shoulder when he raised it too high, but the general soreness seemed to be receding. He'd have to take it easy, whether he wanted to or not, but Gray Hair had to be disposed of. Max locked his office and went downstairs. When he emerged on Chicago Avenue, Gray Hair had regained interest in the racing form. Max walked past Thompson's cafeteria to the corner, poked a cigarette in his mouth, and turned south on Clark Street. Gray Hair betrayed no interest. Max crossed the street, passing within a few feet of the clerkish guy, and went into the drugstore. When he came out with a fresh pack of smokes in his hand Gray Hair was standing sentinel on the Clark Street side of the building. Max walked south on Clark and turned into the Harp Club.

The jukebox was jumping and the long bar was crowded with sweaty, jean-clad men seeking alcoholic respite from their day of toil. Thin-bloused girls, freshly cologned and eager of eye, were circulating among the drinkers looking for live ones. The more brazen were offering a few minutes of relaxation and companionship at bargain rates. Beyond the bar, in a small cleared area surrounded by tables, the more energetic girls were moving vigorously to the blaring beat of the jukebox, giving their partners a taste of pleasures that could be theirs—at matinee prices. Max nodded to several of the girls, waved to the bartender, walked to the rear. He found an unoccupied table and sat down.

A flashy-eyed brunette whose red sweater fitted her C-cup falsies like a ballet dancer's tights came tapping toward his table with the inevitable question: "Wanna buy me a drink, Maxie?"

"Sure, Julie." He tossed her a bill. "I'm drinking scotch."

She tapped away on her high heels, heading for the service flap of the bar. Max got out a fresh cigarette and while lighting it, studied the line-up. Gray Hair had squeezed in near the entrance and was inspecting the foam on a glass of beer. A thin blonde was nudging him, trying to attract his attention. While Max watched, Gray Hair bent toward the girl, spat a sentence or two, and returned to the contemplation of his beer. The girl tossed her head and flounced away, muttering phrases that, although inaudible, were doubtless salty.

Julie returned with Max's scotch and a short mixed drink that looked like Old Lipton's and water. "Where have you been hiding lately, Maxie?" she asked brightly. "Haven't seen you around." She drained her glass in a single swallow and eyed him expectantly. "Gosh, I guess I was thirsty! Want to buy me another?"

Max took a bill from his wallet and folded it so Hamilton could peek at her. "You don't really want another drink, do you, kiddo?"

She blinked, then leaped to the obvious conclusion.

"Guess not, Maxie dear. I'm ready if you are."

He grinned and leaned toward her a little. "Not in August, Julie—it's too damned hot. But there's a gray-haired guy at the other end of the bar who ought to take a trip upstairs. I want to talk to him privately. I'd handle it myself but I've got a bum arm. Think you and Red can work it?"

She nodded quickly. "Which one is he?"

"Don't look now. He's third from the end, in a brown suit, nursing a short beer."

"He's on his way upstairs now, Maxie." She rested a hand on the table and wiggled her fingers. Max put his hand over hers, flattening Hamilton into her hard, moist palm. She smiled and flashed him a wink. "Watch."

Max drank slowly and let his eyes drift back and forth between the bar and the dancers. A few feet from him, a not-so-young brunette in a gaudy print dress was determinedly swinging it with a damp-faced youth, pressing her thin body against him as though trying to steam the creases from his suit. Julie approached a big redheaded guy at the bar and touched his arm. He bent toward her irritably. She spoke briefly, jerking her head once toward the rear. Red nodded, then looked toward Max and grinned. Julie headed for Gray Hair.

The jukebox blared a finale, stopped, shifted gears like molars grinding in a nightmare, and began banging out the *Hot Pretzels* polka. Julie had squeezed in beside Gray Hair and appeared to be resting the front of her sweater on his arm. He jerked his arm away, his face expressing surprise, and reached nervously for his glass of beer.

"Saaay, what d'ya think you're doing, anyway!" Julie's indignant screech cut through the rumble of voices and the blaring polka like a high-speed drill going through aluminum foil. Instantly, those near her moved prudently back.

Gray Hair's reply was an incoherent mumble.

"You did not! You tried to feel me, that's what you did!"

Gray Hair tried to back away from her but succeeded only in looking furtive and guilty. "It's cheap bums like you that give a place like this a bad name!" the girl went on, her voice skipping octaves in rising indignation. "You put your hand on me, just as though I was a common—"

Gray Hair, casting a desperate look over his shoulder and probably realizing he was outclassed, turned as though to flee. The girl clawed at his jacket, effectively negating any attempt at flight. "Ohhh, no, you don't!" she screamed. "You old nasty man, you, you aren't getting away that easy! You insulted me! You—"

Red shouldered his way toward Gray Hair and got into the act. He bunched the front of the clerkish guy's suit jacket in his big fists and demanded, "What the hell you think you're doing to my wife?"

"He tried to feel me!" Julie screeched, managing to sound tearful and distraught. "That's what he did! He put his hand—"

"He did huh?" Red shook him like a housewife ridding a small rug of dust. "You did that to my wife, huh?"

Gray Hair made the mistake of flailing his arms. Red interpreted this as an attempt to strike back, and, with a malevolent grin, chopped a fist at Gray Hair's jaw. The clerkish guy's eyes bulged and he began to slump to the floor.

Max got up quietly, walked to a door at the rear, and went upstairs.

CHAPTER NINE

JULIE UNLOCKED a small bedroom and cleared a wooden chair by pushing the clothes on it onto the floor. Red lugged Gray Hair in as though he were a sack of old rags and propped him on the chair. Gray Hair sputtered and protested feebly and tried to get to his feet. Then he saw Max. He gaped foolishly, then slumped down in the chair like a puppy trying to hide from the conductor on a train.

"You want me to stick around, Max?" Red asked.

"Maybe you'd better," Max decided. "See what he's carrying." Red bent over the clerkish guy and began emptying his pockets. There wasn't much. Some keys, a soiled handkerchief, less than a dollar in small change, a thin wallet, a notebook, the racing form, several pencils, an old CTA transfer, and a few scraps of paper bearing scrawled telephone numbers. Max took the wallet, the notebook, and the scraps of paper. He sat down on the edge of the narrow iron bed and opened the wallet. Gray Hair opened his mouth as though to protest, then thought better of it and glared sullenly at Julie, who was lounging in the doorway, primping her hair.

Red noticed Gray Hair's look and turned toward the girl. "What you loafing here for?" he growled. "Beat it downstairs before them other hookers grab all the live ones!"

"Maybe Max'll need me," she protested.

"I'll let you know if he does!" Red retorted. "Go on, beat it."

"How about it, Maxie?" she asked. "You going to want me?"

"Not for a while," Max told her. "Thanks."

The girl flashed him a smile, tossed one hip insultingly at Red, and slammed the door. Max grinned and returned his attention to the wallet. He deduced from the cards and photos it contained that Gray Hair's name was Samuel P. Toliver, he was 41 years old, lived in Skokie, was a registered Democrat, belonged to Blue Cross, Blue Shield and the Chicago Motor Club, and had a wife and three small kids. Several pages of the notebook were filled with cryptic jottings that suggested an inventory list of some kind; one page was criss-crossed with financial calculations involving the multiplication of large sums by various integers. No final solution to the mathematics was recorded and there seemed very little rhyme or reason to the source of the integers. The phone numbers were equally disappointing; all were for Loop exchanges, but none rang any bells in Max's memory.

"Okay, Toliver," Max said, tossing the wallet back to him. "What's the pitch? Who put you onto me?"

"Aw, go choke!" It was a gutter phrase, charged with frustration, but the expression in his eyes was cringing and frightened, like a dog expecting to be struck.

"Where'd you pick me up?" Max asked.

"I don't know what you're talking about!"

"Maybe he'd like some loose teeth," Red suggested.

"Maybe," Max agreed. He stared at Toliver somberly. You want us to get tough?"

Toliver shivered as though a stream of cold water had trickled down his leg. "Aw, hell—" he muttered. "I didn't do anything to you!"

"You were tailing me," Max said grimly.

"Who says?"

"Maybe you better convince him, Red," Max said. He stood up and walked toward the door.

"What the hell…wait a minute—"

"Yeah?" Max paused in the doorway.

"Don't leave me with this...this—" Toliver eyed Red nervously and choked on a piece of terror-inspired phlegm in his throat.

"It's talk—or else, Toliver," Max said flatly. "I haven't time to kid around."

"So I was tailing you. So what?"

"Who put you onto me?"

"Nobody..."

"What was the big idea, then?" Toliver's fingers twisted like restless snakes. "I...I thought you were somebody I used to know. I wasn't sure, though. I thought I'd follow you and see if...you know, see if you were the guy I used to know."

Max grunted disgustedly and started for the door again.

"Hey, for the love of—don't go! Don't you believe me?"

"Look, Toliver," Max said. "Maybe you think you're playing with kids. You aren't. Hear that jukebox downstairs? My friend can knock holes in you—and you can scream your guts out—and nobody'll even notice. You can play it any way you like, but, if you've got any sense, you'll realize that the fat's in the fire. It's up to you to get yourself out."

Toliver clawed his hands together and swallowed nervously. "Okay, I'll level," he said desperately. "I heard you talking to the store dick in Larsen's, I don't know why I followed you. It was crazy, I guess. I didn't intend to do anything. Honest to God, I didn't! I just thought that if I could find out who you were and what you intended to do, I might...I might—" He shrugged hopelessly.

"You might what?" Max prompted. He sat down on the bed again.

"Hell, it's all mixed up."

"Talk. I'll unscramble it."

"Well, I'm a comparison shopper. You know what that is?" Without waiting for Max's nod, he rushed on: "All the big stores have them, so they can keep track of what everybody else is selling, and I'm out of the store a lot. I go around, check what's being advertised, look at the stuff to see where they bought it and make sure the manufacturers we buy from aren't slipping something to our competitors at lower prices, and—well, things like that. I've been doing that five years now, ever since I had to sell out a business I had. It's a pretty good job, I guess, but I've got a wife and kids and a house out in the suburbs and, gosh, I don't know where the money goes. Either one of the kids is sick, or the furnace has to be repaired, or the car's in the garage getting fixed—always something, see, something to cheat a guy out of enjoying life."

"So you needed dough," Max suggested.

"Sure I needed dough!" Toliver exclaimed bitterly, sounding as though each syllable had been dipped in gall. "A guy with a wife and kids always needs dough!" He looked pleadingly at Max. "If you're married, you know how it is. No matter how much you give them, there's always something else they gotta have. Why, the way things are these days, a man's gotta have two or three jobs—and even then he has a tough time getting ahead unless his wife works too, and I didn't want her to do that, because then the kids would be home alone most of the time. I didn't want to take a chance on them getting to be juvenile delinquents, and still I had to—"

"You were having a tough time," Max interrupted impatiently. "What did you do? Start feeding the ponies?"

"That's about it," Toliver admitted. "Some of the guys at the store were playing them, and, because I could circulate around without punching the time-clock, they asked me to drop in at a book and lay some bets for them. I did it just as a favor, understand. They weren't heavy betters—just a buck or two at a time, you know—but one of them used to hit winners pretty consistently. I started matching some of his bets, just for the hell of it, see, and a couple of times I made out pretty good. After a while it got so I was in the book for an hour or two every afternoon, and I guess I began to feel pretty sure of myself, because I started playing kind of heavy. Then one of the kids needed an operation—and, well, I must have gone nuts. The guys at the book knew me by then of course and I guess they must have figured I was an executive at the store, seeing as how I was in and out all day long, and if I was short a few bucks they'd say it was okay and they'd give me credit. Well, I went nuts, like I said, and first thing I know I'm out on a limb, but good, and the book is pressing me for the dough I owe."

"How much did they get into you for?" Max asked.

"Three grand! I still can't figure it. Honest to God. I was only betting tens and twenties, mostly on long shots to place, and how I ever got in that deep I don't know! But they showed me a ledger and said I owed it, so what the hell was I to do?"

"Whose book were you playing?" Max asked.

"Eddie Schumaker's. He's got a spot in the—"

"I know where it is," Max said. "Eddie's on the square. If he said you owed three grand, you owed three grand. And if Eddie carried you on the tab for that much dough you must have given him a pretty good build-up. Did you tell him you were an executive at Larsen's?"

"Why would I do that? I hardly ever even saw Eddie. A lot of the guys around the book knew that I worked at the store, of course, but I didn't do any bragging. If anybody had asked me what kind of job I had, I'd have told them that I was a comparison shopper, because that's what I am. They could check that—and it'd be the truth, see?"

Max nodded. "But Eddie wanted his dough. So what did you do?"

"What could I do?" Toliver whined. "I didn't have three grand. Hell, after paying for the kid's operation, I hardly had three bucks! The damned horses were running like they had lead boots on, and everything I did was wrong. The more I tried to force my luck, the worse things got. I'd have taken a one-way trip to the garage, but all I carry is a couple thousand in insurance, so—well, I was up against it, wasn't I?"

"Sounds like it," Max agreed. "But you figured a way out?"

"I didn't. I worried myself sick trying to think of some place I could borrow the dough, but you know how it is, when a guy is really in a jam, there's nobody that wants to have anything to do with him—and I was that guy. There wasn't any way out, as far as I could figure, and then this guy called and asked me if I wanted to make a pile of dough—"

"What guy?" Max asked sharply.

"He didn't give me a name. He called me at home and said he'd heard I was a merchandising expert—that's what he called me—and that maybe he could throw some business my way. He wanted to know if I was interested. Naturally, I said yes. Then he wanted to know how familiar I was with the inventory of stock at Larsen's. I told him that I knew about all there was to know in certain lines, because my job was to check and double-check everything for value. When the buyers decide to stock an item, I get a report on it, and right away I try to find out if the other stores have it, and, if so, how much they're charging. I explained the job—and finally he got to the point: How badly did I want to make some dough, some big dough?" Toliver swallowed as though trying to remove a bad taste from his mouth. "Well, I wanted the dough. I wanted the dough worse than Adam wanted that apple. But I almost turned him down. I would have, I think, if I hadn't been scared. I'd heard about guys getting beaten up or shot for not paying their gambling debts, and...and—"

He flapped a hand wearily across his forehead. "I don't know why I'm telling you all this! I must be nuts."

"You're being smart," Max said. "Red's itching to get his hands on you. Aren't you, Red?"

"I ain't killed a guy for nearly a week." Red grinned.

Toliver straightened as though a spasm had tortured his bowels.

"This guy offered you a deal," Max prompted. "You didn't turn him down. What was his pitch?"

"Well, it sounded simple. He gave me a list of some things he was interested in, and he asked me to—"

"What kind of things?" Max interrupted.

"The first time, I remember, he wanted to know about Fischer slips and Strook sweaters. They're quality items that retail at a fairly high price and he wanted to know what kind of an inventory the store had on them. I told him we were loaded. He asked if the store was planning any kind of special sale on those items. I said no. It was early in the fall and if there were any sales, I knew it wouldn't be until after Christmas. Then he asked me a lot of questions about the buyers, the sales personnel in a couple of departments, and things like that. I told him everything he wanted to know. A few days later I got an envelope in the mail. There was $300 in it—no letter, no explanation, nothing. I took it down to the book the next day, and the cashier told me not to worry any more, the pressure was off, I could take my time bringing in the three grand."

"The first payoff," Max commented.

"Yeah, that was the beginning." Toliver squirmed wretchedly. "I didn't know it had anything to do with a racket. You can believe that or not. I thought it might be somebody from one of the other stores, trying to find out what our weak spots were. It wasn't until a month or two later that I heard about the big inventory losses and connected them with things I'd told him. As soon as I realized that he'd been using me to finger likely merchandise for him to steal, I tried to break things off—but, hell, he threatened to let the store know about the dough I still owed Eddie, and, well, I never could quite manage it."

"How long has this been going on?"

"Nearly a year, I guess. He's been calling me two—three times a week lately—"

"You still don't know who he is?"

"I wish I did!" Toliver squared his shoulders and pushed out his chest like a man about to receive a medal. "The bastard's made my life hell! If I could just get to him once, if I could be sure of who he is—"

"Nuts," Max said succinctly. "You knew he was a crook the first time you talked to him. When he talked about big dough and wouldn't give his name, you knew somebody was getting a fast shuffle—but you figured it wouldn't be you. You were worried about your own skin. That's all you've ever been worried about. It's probably why you tried to tail me this afternoon. You were scared somebody'd tumble to your part in the racket and you wanted to warn your pal that—"

"I didn't! Honest to God, I didn't! All I wanted to—"

"Shut up," Max said fiercely. "How do you get in touch with this guy?"

"I don't." Toliver was trembling. "Honest, mister, I never—"

"What if a big deal came up?"

"I still couldn't call him! He always calls me and I—"

"When was the last time he called?"

"Yesterday. I mean, last night."

"He called you at home?"

"Sure. At my house in Skokie."

"What time did he call?"

"A little before seven, it was. I'd gotten home and eaten dinner—and then he called."

"When do you expect him to call again?"

"Not until tomorrow. It's usually every other day now, and—"

"You weren't going to tell him about me until tomorrow?"

"How could I? I don't know his number. I don't even—"

"What about these?" Max pointed to the slips of paper. "Whose numbers are these?"

"They're just numbers for some manufacturer's agents. You can call them and see. I was checking on some things I saw in Shield's this morning, and I called them to find out if they'd cut prices on—"

"Okay, okay," Max interrupted. "Do you know who they've got in the store?"

"I don't know what you mean."

"Who's doing the stealing?"

"I don't know. All I ever did was like I told—"

"Somebody kept track of the clerks, saw that the stuff was wrapped and handed to the right people," Max told him. "Once you knew what was going on, you must have tried to get a line on some of your thieving pals."

"I didn't. Honestly! I was afraid to!"

Max snorted disgustedly. He looked at Red, who had been listening with the perplexed and faintly bored expression of a mambo trotter hearing Brahms, and asked, "What do you think, Red? Does he sound right to you?"

"A pee-wee," Red growled. "Strictly a pee-wee."

"Yeah." Max frowned. "I can't let him run around loose; he might get gassy around the wrong ghees. Tell you what, strip him and keep him here tonight. Tell Julie she's not to let him loose until I give the word. She can get him something to eat from the barbecue next door."

At the word *strip* Toliver came to his feet as though someone had prodded him intimately with an icicle. "You can't do that! You can't keep me here!" He made a frantic leap for the door.

Red stretched an arm out, caught him around the waist and, like a ballplayer making an easy throw to first base, flung Toliver onto the bed. Toliver squealed as the bed's creaking springs flopped him over.

"Get smart for once in your life, Toliver," Max advised. "Once the big boys find out you've talked, you won't have the chance of a celluloid cat in hell. You're a lot safer here than you would be at home. And Julie will take good care of you, real good care of you. Won't she, Red?"

"Sure," Red growled. He was busy taking off Toliver's jacket. "Anything you say, Max...I'll tell her."

Max grinned and walked out.

CHAPTER TEN

IT WAS pushing seven when Max walked into Little Harry's Lounge. The joint was fairly crowded. He spotted two of Harry's dealers at a wall-side table and went over and pulled out a chair. Lefty glanced up, nodded, and went on with what he was telling Chink, who acknowledged Max's presence by lifting two fingers from his glass of beer in a sign of greeting.

"So this damned magazine—*Chicago,* they call it—they come out with a story about floating craps," Lefty was droning, "and what this guy doesn't know about floating craps you could pile higher than the Merchandise Mart. He says when a guy comes into town looking for action, the thing to do is hang around a hotel lounge and wait for a sign. How do you like that? A guy hooking suckers for a game ain't going around with any signs on. Anyway, he says a big limousine comes around to the lounge and everybody gets into it and then the limousine drives them someplace where there's a big vacant warehouse with look-outs and locked doors and blacked windows and crap like that. Hell, anybody that thinks they gotta go to trouble like that to spin their dough down the drain, they oughta get their heads examined. Why, I know six or eight spots, right now—and you do, too, Chink—where all a guy's got to do is snap his fingers and he can have craps, hearts, poker, rum, pinochle—damned near any kinda set-up he wants. And if it's big dough he wants, it's big dough that he gets. Am I right?"

"Yeah, sure, you're right," Chink agreed boredly. He looked at Max. "How's things, Max?"

"So-so," Max said. "Street kind of quiet?"

"Yeah," Lefty said, eyeing Max furtively. "You cooled off yet?"

"That was yesterday," Max told him. "Where'd you hear about it?"

Lefty jerked his shoulder carelessly. "You know how it goes. When a game's going, lots of things get mentioned."

"Sure." Max ordered a round of drinks. "Anybody mention Wally Friedl lately?"

"That jerk." Chink's tone conveyed the impression that Wally Friedl was *persona non grata* in his book.

"Last I heard," Lefty said slowly, "Wally was hustling fur in St. Louis."

"I heard he was around," Max said. "Let me know if you hear anything."

There was silence for a moment, then Lefty began telling about a dame he'd met in a game who had a sable jacket and who took him home with her to a ritzy apartment in the Croydon Hotel. The story highlighted Lefty's sole experience with a woman who hadn't had her hand out, and he told it with a generous sprinkling of salacious detail. Max had heard it before, so he moved sidewise on his chair and studied the customers. It was the usual crowd, rumpled and thirsty and loud. He nodded to several acquaintances, finished his drink, and ordered another.

The lights over the runway blinked on suddenly and a tinny combo on the other side of the bar began rattling out the introduction to *Anything Goes*. Kid Keating, the M. C., appeared on the runway, smiling and bowing affectedly. Max swished a sip of liquor around in his mouth and remembered that he hadn't gotten in touch with Sally Breeze. It was too late to catch her at the apartment. He heard Lefty and Chink get up and leave. He had stopped thinking about Sally Breeze and was wondering how Gwen Collyer had made out with

Little Harry when, hearing a chair scrape behind him, he sensed that someone had joined him at the table.

A moment later Little Harry's voice said, "She's okay, Max. Thanks."

Without turning, Max asked, "Which spot did you give her?"

"She's on after the first strip. After all, she's a newcomer."

"You call Solly?"

"Yeah. He might drop in later."

Max nodded and shifted his chair so he could see Little Harry. "Might?" he repeated.

"Solly didn't sound too interested," Little Henry explained.

The first strip was done by a chunky brunette of too certain years who took off her clothes to the beat of *Sweethearts on Parade* with the careless air of a chimp peeling bananas. Max waited until she got down to a gauze bra, revealing purplish nipples on heavy waxen breasts, then he asked, "Anything new?"

"Mabel called." Harry frowned slightly.

"Yeah?"

"She left a number for you." Harry fished in his shirt pocket, found a slip of paper, passed it across the table. "Any time tonight, she said."

"Thanks."

"Maybe you don't know it, but you put me on kind of a spot."

"How do you figure that?"

"You didn't tell her you was a private dick, did you?"

"Look, Harry," Max said. "What's a private dick? I go around and dig up information for people. I'm not a cop. Anybody with dough can hire me. You called her about the suit because you know I can keep my mouth shut. As far as you're concerned, that's it."

"But you told her she could call you here," Little Harry said, sounding faintly irritated.

"Sure. I like the joint. I'm here a lot. You couldn't refuse to take a phone call for a customer, could you? You don't even know what it's about. Furthermore, you know damned well that I wouldn't walk in here like this if I was bringing heat along with me. I told you yesterday what I was after. You're clean, Harry."

"Hope you're right." Little Harry nodded toward the runway. "Here she comes."

The combo beat out a listless fanfare and Gwen, looking slimmer and taller in the rhinestoned gown, danced gaily down the runway, doing a tricky step that seemed calypso in origin. Her long reddish hair gleamed under the lights as she danced back and forth, kicking her legs and swaying her hips, and the smile that curved her red lips looked genuinely happy and proud. Someone whistled shrilly and several of the customers clapped. Max smiled involuntarily. There was a freshness about her that made her outshine the other broken-down babes in the show. When she reached the finale and loosened up her legs and voice, as well as the maracas with which she was beating out the rhythm, the customers stamped their feet and pounded on the tables. She was reaching them, really reaching them, without undressing like a slut and trying to rub their noses in it. Max caught himself holding his breath and praying that she wouldn't do anything to spoil the spell. She didn't. She danced coyly toward the curtains, flashed a big smile over her shoulder—and slipped away. Someone shouted, "Take 'em off!" There was spontaneous clapping, then the combo banged out a few bars of repeat. But she played it smart. She poked a shoulder through the folds of the curtain, waved an arm—and gave them her big, happy, youthful smile. Period. The customers laughed and loved it.

"Nobody's wowed them like that since the night Mamie's G-string broke," Little Harry commented.

"She's a good clean kid and looks it," Max said. "Anything else would cheapen her, like the others."

"Yeah, maybe that's it," Little Harry agreed. "It's a change, anyway. Hope Solly likes her."

"Unless he's blind and deaf, he'll have to," Max said. "Okay if I go back and see her?"

"Why not?"

Max threaded his way among the tables and went through the door that led to the dressing rooms. When he walked in, Gwen Collyer was saying, "So what if I didn't take it off? The customers liked it, didn't they? Just because—"

The chunky brunette, as naked as when she had bumped off the runway after her strip, was sprawled on a dress-strewn couch with a cigarette in her mouth. "Sure," she replied cattishly, "you went out there and *pretended,* that's what you did! How long you think it'll take them guys to smarten up? If you don't give 'em something to *remember*—"

"I don't care!" Gwen retorted. "The customers liked it—and so did Little Harry!"

"So did I, kiddo," Max said. He patted her bare shoulder and grinned down at the brunette. "Anything Sarah tells you, Gwen, is sour grapes. She's been prancing around naked so long that anybody with clothes on makes her uncomfortable."

"Nuts to you, Maxie," Sarah said good-naturedly. "I was giving the kid some good advice. This is Clark Street, in case she don't know it, and the guys ain't sitting still just for *teasing,* for gosh sake! Two-three nights of what she's doing, and they'll be booing her every time she sticks her nose out. Why, I remember—"

"Sure, sure, you remember the big fire," Max said easily. "Take sixty, will you, Sarah? I want to make some time with Gwen."

"It'll take you more than sixty," Sarah retorted, winking broadly. She got up lazily, gave Max a raised-brow look, and did a mocking bump and grind out of the room.

Max chuckled. "Sarah's a tramp but she means all right," he told Gwen. "She can't understand anything unless it hits her in the face. How do you feel?"

"Wonderful!" She gave him a radiant smile. "Harry says he's going to get me an agent!"

"It's a cinch. Keep the act the way it is and don't cheapen it. Like Sarah says, it isn't Clark Street stuff, but Harry will give you the breaks as long as the customers pound the tables. Solly Franks may have different ideas, of course. He may want to try you in a better joint."

"But Harry's the boss, isn't he?"

"Yes and no. Harry owns the joint, but Solly controls the show. If Solly wants to move you, he'll move you. It's okay for Harry to try new material once in a while, but Solly won't let you waste time here if he thinks he can get more dough for you somewhere else. He wants his ten-percent, and the more he gets for you the more nickels and dimes he collects. He shifts the talent according to what they'll bring—and that's a break for you. It's that way all over."

"Well, I'm not going to worry about it," she said blithely. "You really thought I was good? Gosh, if I'd known you were there, I'd have been nervous!"

"Good enough to make me want a date," Max said. "How about having a steak with me when you finish?"

"Gee, I don't know." She pressed the tips of her fingers against her flat tummy. "I shouldn't. I had a big supper."

"Don't tell me you have to watch that figure of yours!"

"If I don't, maybe nobody else will," She sounded serious.

Max laughed. "I'll pick you up here around one-thirty. It'll be a celebration."

"Well...all right." She smiled. "I guess I ought to celebrate."

"All you have to do now is knock Solly's eyes out, kiddo—and you're in. But this is the easy part. From now on you'll be competing with real talent and—"

"Hey, Max!" The harsh whisper from the doorway stopped him in mid-sentence.

Max whirled and recognized Dippy Jim, the colored boy who did odd jobs around the joint. "What do you want, Dippy?"

The boy rolled his eyes. "Harry says there's a cop looking for you upstairs."

"Yeah? What's he look like, Dippy?"

"Kind of big, Max. A richard, for sure. Harry don't know him."

"He alone?"

"Yeah. He came in a few minutes ago and he's sitting at the bar, looking around. He asked Tolly if he'd seen you. Tolly gave the sign to Harry and Harry told me to tell you that he didn't want no trouble. Want to duck out the back?"

Max thought swiftly. The only plainclothes dicks who might be interested in him were Buck Nehlson, Zike Halloran—and maybe Nehlson's sidekick, Ray Donigan. But Nehlson and Donigan were Vice, so Harry would have known them. It was probably Halloran, which wasn't so bad.

"I'll be up in a minute, Dippy," Max said. "Tell Harry it's okay."

"Sure, Max."

To Gwen, Max explained, "It's something about the killing, I think. Incidentally, I put the cops straight on what happened. In case you're asked, you needn't lie about our having a date yesterday."

"That's good. I was sort of worried," she admitted.

"Don't worry about anything—and don't forget our steak."

"I won't," she promised. She walked beside him to the door. "Be careful, Max."

"Don't say that!" he snapped.

"Why?" She recoiled a step, as though frightened by the fierceness in his voice. "Isn't it all right for me to—"

"Sorry, kiddo. I was reminded of something, I guess." He forced a smile. "See you around one-thirty."

Turning abruptly away so she wouldn't see the flush that the memory of Sally Breeze had brought to his face, he went rapidly upstairs.

CHAPTER ELEVEN

WHEN MAX moved beside Halloran, the Homicide dick set his glass down as though driving a nail. "Where the hell did you come from?" he demanded.

"Hello, sergeant. I was downstairs. Can I buy you a drink?"

"What's downstairs?" Halloran's tone was frankly suspicious.

"Dressing-rooms. One of the girls in the show is a friend of mine."

"You suddenly a stage-door Johnny?" Halloran demanded. "Last night it was Sally Breeze at the Tropic Isle—and now you're trying to make time with a babe here."

"I just wanted to tell Sally what a great act she had," Max said easily. "This girl is a redhead. Very young and choice. Maybe you remember talking to her yesterday, Gwen Collyer. The girl who found me in her apartment."

"What's she doing here?"

"Harry's giving her a try-out. She's pretty good, too. Want to stick around and catch the show?"

"Hell, no," Halloran growled. "You think I'm a private dick? I got no time to sit around joints like this."

"Suit yourself. I thought you wanted to talk to me."

"I do." Halloran drained his glass and jerked his head toward the door. "I've got a car outside. It's quieter."

When they were in the car, Halloran got out a cigar, struck a match, and, watching Max over the yellow flame, said in an odd tone of voice, "I hear you got shot."

"Nothing serious," Max said. He moved his arm gingerly. "Bastard winged me."

"Could have killed you."

"Sure," Max agreed. "Lucky for you he didn't."

Halloran didn't notice the thrust. "According to the papers, it happened around Arlington and Clark."

"That's right."

"Real early this morning, huh?"

"Three-fifty." Max had an idea what was coming and he braced himself inwardly.

"What were you doing there, Max?"

Halloran asked the question quietly, but Max sensed that he was coiled tightly inside, ready to lash out like a steel spring. "You read my statement, didn't you?" Max sparred.

"I checked," Halloran admitted. He exhaled a thin plume of smoke. "The cop who took it was green," he added judiciously. "If he knew you like I know you, he could have saved himself the trouble of writing it down."

Max hesitated. Halloran was a smart cop. He undoubtedly knew Sally Breeze's address and suspected that Max's presence in the vicinity at that hour meant that he had been visiting Sally. But if Halloran was carrying a torch for the blonde, it would do Max no good to admit the truth. There had been enough sparks between him and Halloran, and to confess that he'd been trespassing on the cop's dream-stuff would mean open warfare. For all Max knew, maybe Halloran had been helping Sally with the rent.

"You damned cops have no imagination," Max said slowly, trying to give Halloran the impression that he was struggling with a great inner conflict. "Sure, I gave the district cop a line. I had to. But I leveled with you last night. You ought to have imagination enough to put two and two together."

"I put them together," Halloran said sourly, "and I don't like the answer I get."

"Why not? Hell, I was giving your girlfriend a break."

"A break! Why, you—!"

"Wait, Halloran. Don't go flipping your lid until you get the whole picture. Maybe I should have given it to you last night, but when I walked in on Sally you jumped all over me, and then you acted like you were soft for the kid—so I let it slide. I didn't want to embarrass her, and I didn't want to needle you, so—"

"What the hell are you trying to say?" Halloran demanded. "If you're figuring out another run-around to hand me—"

"I'm not," Max said candidly, making up his mind. "Remember what I told you last night about my sitting in the cafeteria and seeing some drops made?"

"So you saw some drops made," Halloran's mouth twitched cynically.

"Sally made one of them."

Halloran bit his cigar savagely. "I ought to punch your teeth down your lying throat, Keene."

"I figured you'd take it like that," Max said. He pointedly ignored the balled fist that Halloran seemed to be itching to toss. "I don't know how crazy you are about the girl, but you ought to be cop enough to recognize facts. What I'm giving you now are facts. If you'd rather just blow off like a dumb Irishman, go ahead—but sooner or later you're going to have to listen."

Halloran slowly unclenched his fist. "Okay, you wise bastard," he said tensely. "I'm listening—but you better make it damned good!"

"I spotted Sally in the cafeteria," Max said carefully. "She was wearing a burnt-orange outfit and she came in with two packages. She's a sexy-looking kid, so I took a good look at her—and I remembered her. Any guy would. Later in the afternoon I had some business on Arlington Place, and I happened to see Sally come out of her building, carrying a hatbox. She had on a different outfit, but I was certain that it was the same girl—so I tailed her to the Tropic Isle. I talked to Danny Green, caught the show, and then went to her dressing-room with the intention of pressuring some facts about the racket from her."

Max paused, fumbled for a cigarette. Halloran maintained a flinty silence.

"I was sore because of the way you jumped me," Max continued, "and I was tempted to spill what I knew right in front of both of you, because it was pretty obvious that she'd hit you hard—but I kept quiet about her involvement. I'm not a complete heel, in spite of what you think, and she impressed me as a real nice kid. But while I was telling you about the cafeteria episode, I made a point of mentioning that one of the droppers was a good-looking blonde, about her size and weight—so she knew that I'd pegged her. That's why she suggested that you go and get the coffee, Halloran. She wanted a chance to talk to me alone, and, as soon as you left, she admitted that I'd pegged her right and said she'd explain everything if I came to her apartment some time after one-thirty."

Halloran grunted. Max glanced at him quickly, but Halloran merely nodded impatiently.

"After I left you," Max went on, "I grabbed some chow, then headed for her apartment. It was kind of early when I got there, so I waited in my car, figuring there was net use buzzing her bell until the time she said. While I was waiting, a sedan drove up and dropped her off. I heard her call the driver 'Buck' when she thanked him. Then I spotted the plates and noticed a radio antenna on the right rear fender. I waited a few minutes, then I went up to her apartment."

"So?" Halloran growled.

"She told me about the whole set-up." Max repeated in detail what Sally had told him about her early struggles and the way a phone call had paved the way for her job at the

Tropic Isle. "She impressed me as a hell of a nice kid," Max said sincerely. "She'd had a lot of tough breaks and she'd gotten sucked into a racket without quite realizing what was going on. In the eyes of the law she's guilty as an accomplice, of course, but she deserves a fair shake, Halloran. I'm convinced that she told me the truth—all of it—and it wasn't easy for her to tell it to me, a total stranger. Maybe she'd have told you about it if you didn't always go around barking like a cop with a tin shield nailed to his can."

"What about the shooting?" Halloran demanded, ignoring the crack.

"It was like I told the district cops," Max said. "Incidentally, Sergeant Nehlson of Vice has been giving me a hard time. It seems the sedan I spotted was his."

Halloran was silent a long time. Max could feel him sorting through the details, weighing and filing them, as mechanically and emotionally as a coin counter separating nickels and dimes. The cigar in Halloran's mouth had died and his lips rolled and chewed at it, torturing it absently. While he reached a decision.

"How'd the *Trib* get the story?" Halloran asked finally.

"Nehlson tried to pressure me into changing my statement," Max told him. "I thought he might have an angle I hadn't tumbled to, so I let a few words drop to Abe Simon. I haven't seen a paper. How'd he play it?"

"Page one," Halloran said. "There's no doubt about it being Nehlson's car?"

Max grinned. "You ever had anybody throw lead at you unexpectedly, Halloran?"

"Once."

"Did you stop to see what color eyes he had?"

"Hell, no. I ducked fast and grabbed for my gun. Killed him, too."

"That's what I mean. I ducked damned fast and I didn't stick my head up to look at plates. But it was a dark sedan—I didn't know it was Nehlson's, of course—but it had to be somebody who knew Sally had a date with me. I figured he had come back and waited."

"So there's a chance that Nehlson's clean," Halloran commented.

"There's a chance that he lives on five grand a year, too," Max said dryly, "but I doubt it."

Halloran scowled. "You haven't said it exactly," he said in the cold tones of a man who likes things neatly arranged in his mind, "but you're implying that the person who shot at you may be the one who killed the Parreo girl. They're all in the same racket." He moistened his lips. "Sally, too."

"Maybe you can add it up differently?"

By the way the big cop suddenly jerked the cigar from his mouth and eyed it distastefully, Max knew that Halloran was close to a decision—and it was one that didn't sit well on his stomach. Halloran threw the cigar out the window and turned on the car's ignition.

"We're going somewhere?" Max asked.

"Yeah."

"Where?"

Without answering, Halloran swung the car around and headed north. Max lit another cigarette. When they reached Division Street, Halloran said abruptly, "I've been a cop nearly twenty years, Keene, long enough to know that anybody can have an angle. Most people do, that includes Sally. As much as I like her, I'm a cop, first and always. I'm going to question her...in your presence...and I'm going to find out if there's any truth in what you say."

"Don't be tough on her. She's a nice kid."

"Asking questions and demanding honest answers isn't getting tough," Halloran snapped. "Either it's like you say—

or it isn't. And if some crooked bastard's got a string on her, I'm going to squeeze the mud out of his dirty rotten heart."

Max had expected Halloran to be incredulous, even angry, but he hadn't expected the blaze of fury that seemed to be seething through the big cop's brain. Though there was no necessity for haste, Halloran drove as though he had a lead foot and disregarded other cars completely. Max felt sorry for Sally. Halloran's mood was an ugly one. He probably intended to barge in on her, shaking a sword of righteous anger, and try to make a third degree chamber out of her dressing room. If he did, he was a damned fool. Maybe he was crazier about the girl than Max had suspected. It was beginning to look as though Max had made a *faux pas,* but there wasn't much he could do about it now. Hell, Max decided, it was something that had to be faced sooner or later. Might as well let Halloran blow himself out...

Halloran yanked at the wheel savagely and kicked at the brake. The car swooped toward the curb and screeched to a stop beside the Tropic Isle's family entrance. Halloran was out and walking on the sidewalk before Max could unlatch the door on his side. Max had gotten out and was coming around the car when Danny Green came out of the Tropic Isle's front entrance, looking as though he'd just caught a bartender dropping quarters into the sink. He looked anxiously up and down Clark Street, then turned and saw them. He strode toward them, motioning with one hand.

"What's eating him?" Halloran muttered.

"Some big deal," Max said. "Probably needs a light fixed."

"Hey, you guys!" Danny Green cried. He looked genuinely agitated. "What the hell did you do with Sally?"

"Sally!" Halloran rasped. "Isn't she here?"

"She *should* have been here an hour ago!" Green said angrily. "We got a good crowd and I've been calling her for the last half-hour. Everybody's asking for the damn snake and the show's nearly over and the little bitch hasn't even phoned to let—"

Halloran's fist put a period to the sentence. Green stumbled backward, clutching at his face, and rammed against the building. Without giving him a second glance, Halloran snapped, "Something's happened to her! Get in, Max." When the car was rolling again, Halloran muttered, "I guess I shouldn't have poked the crumb, but nobody's calling Sally a bitch unless he can damned well prove it." The car careened crazily as though to give emphasis to his words.

"For cryin' out loud, Halloran," Max protested, holding to the door handle so he wouldn't bump his arm, "take it easy! She could be just delayed, you know."

"You don't know Sally," Halloran snapped. "She's usually ready and waiting long before her cue. She always fed the snake first, before she even started to dress. If she hasn't shown, it's something serious."

"She isn't in her apartment," Max said, suddenly remembering.

"How do you know?"

"I called her a couple of times. No one answered."

"I'll check anyway," Halloran said grimly.

As the car ground to a stop, Max noticed that someone had replaced the shattered glass in the building's door with a plywood panel. Without waiting for Max, Halloran leaped to the sidewalk and headed into the building. Max slammed the car door and hurried after him.

When Max reached the third floor, the door of Sally Breeze's apartment was open and Halloran was standing as though frozen in the foyer off the living room. Max pushed against Halloran, trying to see into the room.

Halloran shoved Max back violently. Then Halloran began to curse.

CHAPTER TWELVE

SHE WAS lying on the big couch, her blond head pillowed on one outflung arm and her naked body twisted as though she had been trying to rise. A hard lump choked Max's throat as he looked down at her. It was easy to visualize what had happened. Someone had entered, someone with a key, for her robe lay on the floor exactly where Max had flung it. The purplish bruises about the white column of her neck showed where the killer had grasped her, squeezing the life from her body. She had struggled, sleepily, ineffectively. The killer had been strong, determined—and efficient. He had flung her lifeless body to the couch and then, like a bloodthirsty wild beast, apparently had bitten her flesh. It would seem the act of a crazed man, a man whose rotten brain concealed a perversion infinitely more horrible than a mere lust to kill.

Max, feeling sick at heart and at stomach, turned away.

"You've got an alibi, I suppose," Halloran said in a voice like ground glass. His face was the color of bleached cotton.

"I don't know," Max said dully. "I didn't kill her. You ought to know that."

"How would I know?" Halloran demanded. "You were here last night. It could have happened then. Maybe you came for conversation—sure, that's a hell of a good excuse—but you could have tried to get your hands on something besides information. She was no pushover. She would have told you off and fought and—"

"Knock it off, Halloran," Max said wearily. "Use your head for something besides keeping your eyes apart. Look at her robe. Does it look like somebody tore it off her? Look at the furniture. If she put up a fight, it wasn't much of an effort. She was lying there naked, asleep probably, and whoever came in had a key. It was somebody she knew, somebody who rated a key to her apartment. It looks to me like a hot flame in her life tried to plug me—and then came back to take care of her."

"Who?" The word dripped sarcasm. "Nehlson?"

"As easily him as me," Max snapped. "Why not ask him?"

"I intend to," Halloran said grimly. "But I keep remembering that you were on the premises when Helen Parreo got it—and you were here last night. Maybe they were in on the same racket, but it's a hell of a coincidence when a private dick just *happens* to be—"

The homicide detail arrived from downtown at that moment, giving Max a chance to fade into the background. He sat down out of their way and waited until an assistant coroner had okayed removal of the body and Halloran began busily directing the photographers and crime lab men. Max watched his chance, then edged toward the door and went quietly downstairs.

When he reached the street, he strode east to Clark and climbed aboard the first streetcar that came along. It was a Clark-Wentworth car and he rode it to Chicago Avenue. His office building was locked for the night. He rang the night bell, waited, then rattled the doors impatiently until the watchman appeared. When the door was unlocked, he ran up to the second floor. Josie, the chubby cleaning woman, was swinging a broom in Dr. Chakoian's dental office. Max responded shortly to her greeting and hurried down the darkened corridor. Without bothering to turn on the lights in his office, he went to his desk and turned the phone so that light from the street would illuminate its dial faintly.

He checked with the answering service first. He had had four calls, three of which were identical: *Sergeant Nehlson called.*

The first of Nehlson's calls had been recorded at 5:17, the second at 5:35, the third at 5:50. The fourth call was from Tom Ames, requesting that Max contact him at a State number. Max jotted the number down and dialed it. It rang for two full minutes. No answer. Cursing softly, Max got out the slip of paper that Little Harry had given him and spun the dial again. The phone rang six or seven times before the receiver at the other end was lifted and a voice said, "Hello?"

"Who is this?" Max asked cautiously.

"Well, who do you want?" There was an odd half-male, half-feminine quality to the voice, and it seemed curiously familiar.

"Mabel told me to call this number," Max said carefully.

"Oh, she did, did she?" The voice sharpened a little, like a jealous wife's, and Max tried to visualize the person behind it.

"Yeah."

"Well, you've got the wrong number!"

Memory clicked. Max said quickly, "Verne, this is Max."

"Max?" The wire hummed.

"You saw me at Mabel's yesterday. You lifted a gray suit—"

"Really, you've got the wrong number!" There was a sharp click, then the line hummed emptily.

Max muttered a pithy commentary on the habits and habitat of she-men and redialed the number. It rang twenty times. Either Verne had hung up and swished out, or the long-fingered nance was stubbornly refusing to answer. Max dropped the receiver onto its cradle and lit a cigarette.

For a while, his thoughts wandered like a river in meadowland. Why had Helen Parreo been killed? Because she had been seen with him? No, that wouldn't hold. Even if he'd been pegged as a private dick, it wouldn't have worried them that much. Perhaps she had been a sinker. That was possible...but foolish. So what was the motive? Possession of the day's loot? Hell, all they had to do was reach in the car and take it. To shut her up, then? Sure. She handled a drop and knew about the racket. But *who* was afraid she'd talk *to whom?*

And Sally. That didn't add at all. Assume Nehlson had been the gunman who had tried to mow him down. Okay, in that event Nehlson had known about her date with him. He would also have known, or have suspected, the reason for the date. So if Nehlson had wanted to shut her up, he'd have done it before she could have kept the date. Letting her talk, then trying to kill him—and then killing her—hell, it made practically no sense at all. Unless Nehlson had been soft for her, had gotten into a sweat when he noticed the light go out, and had determined to kill them both because he thought she'd double-timed him. It was a sticky thought. Max considered it dispassionately and decided against it. Nehlson was assigned to Vice. He was used to dealing with women of easy virtue, hookers of every kind, duplicity of high and low caliber. Sally was a looker—but still just a dame. Even if she'd hit him where he lived—and he had caught her in the act with another ghee—he'd be more apt to vent his rage on her than on the fellow. So the racket was back of everything. The knifing of Helen Parreo. The shooting. The strangling of Sally Breeze...

Max sighed and thought about the racket. Obviously, heavy money was involved. But not enough to interest any one of the big syndicates. Most likely it was a local operation, strictly dependent upon the existence of job-hungry girls and weak characters like Samuel Toliver. It was boosting—done with finesse, but still boosting, essentially a small-time fly-by-night racket that couldn't last forever. So the mind behind the racket was a hipster who knew his way around, one who was betting on grabbing a pile for himself before the big kiss-off—yet one who was a shrewd organizer. Nehlson was probably unscrupulous and undoubtedly interested in feathering his own nest, but the racket didn't fit Nehlson's temperament. Max could imagine Nehlson plunging his hand into a prostitute's purse, but he couldn't imagine him quietly organizing a widespread operation of small-time thievery.

There was the biting, too. Max remembered the tooth--torn flesh he had seen—and shuddered. A money-hungry psycho. A killer of girls—and a lousy marksman. Too bad Sally hadn't had her snake handy.

Max straightened, remembering the snake. Impulsively, he reached for the phone, asked Information for the number of the Tropic Isle, and called it. When Danny Green's voice came on, Max said, "Danny, this is Max Keene."

There was a moment of silence, then Green said vehemently, "Tell that two-bit cop friend of yours that I'm going—"

"Danny, listen!" Max interrupted. "We found Sally."

"Well, tell her to take her act and stick it right straight—"

"Listen, Danny. She's dead. Sally's dead."

"Dead?" Green's voice dropped several octaves. "You kidding?"

"No. Someone killed her last night."

Danny made a choking noise and then somberly said, "Hell, that's tough...that's really tough." There were a few seconds of silence. At last he said, "She was a good kid, a real good kid."

"I know she was," Max agreed softly.

"I better get my bid in for a new act," he said in a low, almost empty manner. He was obviously quite shaken. "Thanks for letting me know, Max. Come around and I'll buy you a drink—"

"Danny—has anybody fed the snake?"

"How would I know?"

"Well, it's in your basement and somebody ought to take it to the zoo or feed it or—"

"It is like hell in my basement."

"She kept it there, didn't she?"

"Most of the time she did. But it isn't there now."

Max frowned. "Are you sure?"

"I should lie about a snake?" Green sounded offended. "If there's anything I got no use for, it's a damned snake that crawls around girls and—"

"Danny—what happened to it?"

"How do I know? I went down a couple of hours ago— and no snake. I figured she'd moved the act without notice and I was going to call her agent tomorrow and raise hell because she didn't even—"

"Danny. Listen a minute. This is important. She didn't take the snake with her last night. I don't think so, anyway. All she had was a hatbox. So the snake must have been there this morning. Ask if anybody saw it, will you?"

"Hey, you think it crawled out of the box and—!" Alarm flooded Green's voice.

"It should be there. Ask, will you? I'll hang on."

"Okay, okay."

Max lit a cigarette nervously and tried to imagine the snake coiled within the capacity of a hatbox. It was impossible. A hatbox wasn't large enough—or strong enough, either. It had to be in the basement. And if it was loose down there it was hungry and dangerous...

Green's voice came back.

"Manny says a guy picked it up this morning." Green sounded greatly relieved. "He forgot to tell me."

"What guy?"

"He don't know. Says the guy said he was a vet and that the snake was sick. Manny showed the guy how to get down to the basement and the guy took the snake out, box and all.

You know, you scared the hell out of me, Max. I thought for a minute it might have been crawling around down there while—"

"Find out what the guy looked like!" Max interrupted.

"Big guy with glasses. That's all Manny remembers."

"What was he wearing?"

Green's voice turned away and Max could hear him shouting, "Hey, Manny, what'd the guy have on?" Max heard a far-away mumble, then Green said, "All Manny noticed was a kind of dirty white jacket. You think somebody heisted it, Max?"

"Looks like it."

"Who'd be nuts enough to heist a damn snake?" Green's tone was derisive. "That's what I'd call being really hard up—"

Max hung up feeling confused and baffled. No one except her killer could have known that Sally would have no further use for the snake. But, as Danny Green had quipped, who could be nuts enough to heist a snake? It had value, sure, as a zoo exhibit, as a prop for another exotic dancer, maybe, but it made a hell of a keepsake, an even worse pet. It wasn't worth stealing. But the killing of Helen Parreo had been needless. And the murder of Sally Breeze had been foolhardy. It made a picture, but damned if he could see it.

Max's arm throbbed, reminding him that he had been sitting stiffly for a long time. It was nearly midnight. Nehlson was looking for him. Halloran would be looking for him. And so would the killer. But he couldn't run forever...

He had made up his mind to check Nehlson's alibi at the Melody Bar and was rising from his chair when the phone rang. He reached for it—and stopped with his hand in mid-air. It might be Nehlson. It might be Halloran. The phone rang again. It might be Ames, too. The phone rang a third time. Max lifted the receiver.

"Yes?" he murmured.

"Max? Oh, I'm so glad I caught you!"

He recognized Gwen Collyer's voice and some of the tension went out of him. "You aren't through work already, are you, Gwen?"

"I'm through, Max—for good. That's why I called, to tell you there's nothing to celebrate. I'm going back to Kansas City, Max. On the next train." She was talking rapidly, trying to be aloof and unconcerned, but there was a brittleness in her voice like that of a little girl trying not to cry over the breakage of a favorite doll. "So thanks for everything, Max. I'll send you a card when—"

"What happened, Gwen?"

"I just didn't make the grade, I guess. Anyway, it's not your fault. I—"

"Gwen, tell me what happened! Harry liked the act. So did the customers—"

"But Solly Franks didn't. Period." She tried to suppress a sniffle. Filtered through the receiver, it sounded like a rustle of dry paper. "He...he wouldn't even let me finish the day. He told Harry to...to get rid of me right away...and Harry paid me and sent me home. But it wasn't your fault. It's me, I guess. Honest, Max—" Her voice went away for a moment, then returned fleetingly. "Wait a minute. Someone's at the door."

Max heard an indistinct mumble...then a short, sharp scream, ending in throttled silence.

A moment later someone replaced the receiver.

Horror rendered him immobile for a second, then realization sent him rushing downstairs. The building's doors had been re-locked. He wasted a couple of minutes shouting and searching for the watchman. When the doors were, opened, finally, he ran for his Pontiac and sent it racing, toward East Chestnut. Lights were visible in Gwen Collyer's apartment. He leaped from the car without turning off the ignition and headed for the entrance. The inner door was locked. Cursing, he jabbed buttons indiscriminately until the door release began chattering. He shouldered the door back, started upstairs—and remembered his gun. He got it out, ran up the remaining stairs, clicked off the safety as he strode down the corridor with fear', clutching at his stomach. A yellow bar of light lay across the carpeting outside her door. He flung the door back, stepped in, the gun tight against his side—and stared blankly around at the deserted room.

The rhinestoned calypso gown lay across a chair as though flung there in despair. A battered make-up case stood unopened on the floor. A pair of narrow, high-heeled pumps lay beside the telephone stand, mute evidence of where she had been standing while talking to him. There was a faint trace of cologne and cigarette smoke on the quiet air. He located a crystal ashtray near the telephone. A thin bluish plume was rising lazily from it as though calling attention to a butt not completely extinguished. And a crumpled handkerchief lay on the floor near the door.

He was staring at the crumpled handkerchief when he half-felt, half-sensed the rush of a large body behind. He started to turn...then a black pool yawned and he dove headfirst into it.

CHAPTER THIRTEEN

A VOICE said, "Wonder where the dame is?"

Another voice said, "Never mind the dame."

Max groaned and opened his eyes. A glittery puff of fabric swam into focus. He stared at it and struggled with memory. It came to him slowly: Calypso gown. So he was still in Gwen's apartment. He groaned and tried to twist his body. The arms of a chair clasped him. His arm arched—and so did his head. In spite of the pain, he lifted his head slowly. Two men were on the couch, smoking cigars and watching him. One was Sergeant Nehlson; the other was younger, probably his partner, Ray Donigan. A deep sigh rose from within Max and splashed into the silence.

"You hit him too hard," Nehlson said in the cool tone of an expert criticizing another's handiwork.

"Hell, he had a rod," Donigan retorted.

"It was still too hard."

"He's okay now."

"Don't rush him," Nehlson said. "We got plenty time."

Max swallowed painfully and moistened his lips. "You bastards," he muttered.

"He don't like us," Donigan said. He nudged Nehlson. "Hear that, Buck?"

"Shut up, Ray. I'm trying to figure something out."

Donigan shrugged and eyed Max quizzically.

"What'd you do with her?" Max demanded.

"Do with who?" Donigan asked.

"Gwen Collyer! If you bastards have—"

"He means the dame," Donigan explained helpfully. "That must be the name of—"

"Shut up, Ray." To Max, Nehlson said, "You were the only one here, Keene. We came up on your heels."

Max stared at them. Gwen wasn't there. As the whole panic-tinged moment flooded back, he swung his head around involuntarily, searching for the door of the bathroom. It was closed. A lump clogged his throat. Hoarsely, he asked, "She isn't...in there?"

"Nobody's there," Nehlson said. He shook his head slightly and ash from his cigar drifted down onto the lapel of his flannel jacket.

"There's just us," Donigan said, "just us three lovers."

"Did you look?" Max insisted.

"Show him, Ray," Nehlson said. He continued to regard Max seriously as though he was a scientist considering a glass slide for exhibit.

Donigan got up reluctantly, opened the bathroom door, and turned on the light. It was obvious that there was nothing in the tiled cubicle except a few towels and the standard fixtures. Donigan bowed mockingly, snapped off the light, and returned to the couch. "I guess I did hit him too hard," he commented. "He's nuttier than a fruitcake."

"What's going on, Keene?" Nehlson asked, ignoring his partner. "Why the big rush getting over here? And who'd you expect to find?"

Max frowned. "Where'd you pick me up?" he asked.

"Chicago and Clark," Nehlson said candidly. "We've been buzzing around all night, trying to spot you. Donigan thought you might be holed in your office, and we were on our way to check. You came out on the run and headed for here." He shifted his cigar. "Donigan came onto you kind of suddenly and you had a rod in your mitt."

"You couldn't have snatched her, then," Max muttered, more to himself than to them.

"Look, Keene," Nehlson said casually. "You've been a thorn in my tail all day. Maybe I was kind of rough on you this morning, but you'd flip your lid too if somebody made a stupid mistake and you got put on the pan because of it. I figured you for a dumb private dick who'd gotten himself in a mess and who'd grabbed a license number out of the air to take some of the heat off himself. It happened to be my license number—and I got sore—and apparently I made matters worse by using some corny pressure." He chewed the cigar a moment. "Hell, I never thought you were serious; if I had, I wouldn't have let you out of my sight."

"Now you're convinced, I suppose," Max said acidly.

"Just about," Nehlson admitted. "Donigan and I were in and out of a lot of joints tonight, looking for you, and I talked to quite a few of the boys. They say you're a smart private dick, a little reckless and stubborn, but you're not a chiseler, not a liar, and definitely haven't got a hand out. In other words, the vote was that you're more right than wrong, so I'm convinced that you must have been shooting at something when you gave that story to the Trib. What I want to know is: Who the hell are you shooting at? It can't be me. I never saw you until this morning. But you've gotten me into plenty of hot water, for no reason apparently. I think I rate an explanation."

"Will you answer a couple of questions, Nehlson?"

"Sure."

"Didn't you pick Sally Breeze up at the Tropic Isle last night and drive her home?"

"I did." Nehlson nodded.

"Where'd you go from there?"

"After I dropped her off?" Nehlson sucked on his cigar. "Hell, Donigan and I cruised around and stopped at a few dozen joints. What's that got to do with you?"

"Donigan's your alibi?"

"Donigan and the joints." Nehlson smiled faintly around his cigar. "They aren't apt to forget, either. It was collection night." He eyed Max narrowly. "You spotted me when I dropped the blonde, so you figured I might have come back."

"Didn't you?" Max snapped.

"No."

"I still think it figures."

"Maybe I can give you a few good arguments." Nehlson smiled slightly. "First, I like dough better than I do dames. Donigan and I are assigned to Vice, but Vice assignments are always temporary. We've got about four-five years to make a stake, then we'll be shifted. Like Halloran. He used to be on Vice, now he's on Homicide. But I'm not like Halloran; I'm not a cop for my health. Dames are a dime a dozen and last night was our night to make collections. The dough involved was worth more than any sixteen blondes, and we tended strictly to business. We hit the Tropic Isle and, because the blonde happened to be going our way, we gave her a lift. On the way, we were kidding about the horses and she said she expected a hot tip in the morning. Still kidding, I asked to be cut in on it. She said sure, she'd call me in the morning. As a matter of fact, I took her phone number and buzzed her a couple of times just before noon. She didn't answer and neither Donigan nor I have seen her since."

Nehlson sounded on the level, but Max grunted skeptically.

"If you want a better argument," Nehlson continued, "think about this: A guy took you by surprise and fired three shots. If I'd been behind that gun, you'd be dead. I was a pistol expert in the Marines. I've got medals to prove it."

Nehlson was convincing, damned convincing. But what swayed Max most was the fact that time was running out and Nehlson and Donigan were obviously determined to hold him until he came through with a solid explanation. Besides having a bum arm, Max was at a double disadvantage. It was two against one—and they were armed. He had to take a chance on Nehlson…

Max began with the killing of Helen Parreo. He went over it quickly, but with enough detail to show the mechanics of the racket. Donigan looked increasingly skeptical but Nehlson listened intently. Max described Sally Breeze's murder. Nehlson looked surprised and Donigan began to scowl. It was obvious that neither had heard of her death. Max told them about Gwen Collyer's phone call, the scream he had heard—and the quiet click of the receiver. Donigan stared at the phone, then got up and began studying the room.

Nehlson was silent for a while after Max finished. Dropping the cigar into the ashtray, he said, "Chances are that the Collyer girl is okay. If they'd intended to kill her, they'd have killed her."

"Why snatch her, then?" Max demanded.

"A good question," Nehlson admitted. "She lived here next to the Parreo kid. Maybe she was in on the racket. She might even be the killer. The phone call could have been a fake, a way of fading from the scene—"

"For God's sake, Nehlson—" Max said disgustedly.

"I'm thinking like a cop, not like a private dick," Nehlson explained. "Here's another angle: Gwen Collyer was on the ropes and needed a job. Suppose someone offered her a hunk of dough to do a fade. Maybe she knew something—or might remember something. The dough would be tangible— and you and the job at Little Harry's would be expendable."

"If that's thinking like a cop, I'm glad I—" Max began.

"Okay. Let's assume the snatch was on the level. That means it was worth a lot of trouble. Getting a girl, especially a live one, out of a building is a lot harder than you think. It had to be handled slick and fast. That means they were familiar with the premises, knew their—"

"Maybe she's still in the building," Donigan suggested.

"Not a chance." Nehlson shook his head positively. "While we were sitting here waiting for Keene to get conscious, they had plenty of time to hustle her out the back and down the alley. And we've been gassing quite a while, too, don't forget. They've had nearly an hour and a half to make the snatch good."

"So we sit here and gas some more!" Max cried.

"We're not wasting time; we're using our heads," Nehlson told him. "You're used to a one-man private-shield operation, Keene. Forget that. I'm interested in this now and Donigan and I can broaden the field. Whoever it is, you must have gotten pretty close to them. Here's another thought: This snatch may be a completely diversionary action; it may be intended as a means of getting you off the trail for a day or two. My guess is that the killer is getting a little nervous, is afraid you may tumble to him—and is trying to clutter up your thinking."

"It couldn't be any more cluttered up than it is!" Max said bitterly.

"Frankly, what interests me most is this biting business," Nehlson said slowly. "A vice cop runs across a lot of screwy perversions and usually, when we pin them down, they're indulged in mostly by people who have been sexually repressed. When they start letting go, they blow up completely and the sex urge becomes uncontrollable. Outwardly, they act and look like normal human beings, of course, but deep inside they're boiling like white-hot lava. Usually they require abnormal triggering—masochism, sadism, necrophilia, things like that—"

"Like that guy with the whip," Donigan interrupted.

"Sure. Whips, needles, razor blades, paddles—they're common. Ask any of the hookers on the street. Biting is kind of unusual, though. They had a run of it in England a couple years ago, but we haven't had any of it here. My guess is that the guy to look for is someone who has been sexually repressed—or grossly unsuccessful—and who has sadistic tendencies. Take the Parreo killing. He slugged you and beat up on her. It excited him. At the time he may not even have realized what he was doing, but he ripped off her clothes and used his teeth on her. To us, it's horrible; it may even have seemed horrible to him, later. But at the time the compulsion dominated him and he couldn't control it any more than you can control the beating of your heart. See what I'm driving at?"

"In plain words, he's a murderous psycho bastard!" Max said flatly.

"Not necessarily murderous—and not necessarily a he," Nehlson corrected. "It could be a woman, you know, with the wrong kind of hormones. The act was sadistic, sure, but the killing was possibly an accidental result, not the intended end. Helen Parreo may have fought back, tried to scream. The same with Sally Breeze. She was a dancer—and dancers are muscular. She may have given him quite a fight. If she'd fainted—or, as Confucius say, relaxed and enjoyed it—he might have been content with a couple of kisses—and she'd be alive."

"In that case, let's hope Gwen fainted!" Max exclaimed.

"Even if she didn't, I think she has a good chance," Nehlson told him. "He was pressed for time, remember. He probably realized that she was talking to you on the phone and that you'd be hot to find out what had happened. He had to get her and himself out without being spotted—and without leaving a trail. By the time he did that, he'd had a chance to cool off a little, which was a break for her. Unless she tries to fight him, arousing him anew, he might even regret the snatch and let her go," "So what do we do?" Max demanded.

"Right now, nothing," Nehlson said. "Donigan and I will check around, but the thing for you to do is to go home and sit by—"

"Go home?" Max echoed incredulously. "Are you crazy? I've got to—"

"You've only got one thing to do and that's to use your head," Nehlson said grimly. "You sound like this girl is important to you. If she is, you'll be giving her a break by doing exactly nothing. She may have been snatched to put pressure on you, in which case you'll get a call. If she was snatched for another reason, well..." Nehlson shrugged, "...let's face it, she's dead by now and somebody will find her body. Until then, there isn't anything to be accomplished by your chasing around looking for her. Go home, get some sleep—and wait."

"Go home, get some sleep!" Max repeated. "Hell!"

"It's good advice," Nehlson got up. "Better give him his rod, Ray."

"Sure. I forgot." Donigan took Max's .38 from his jacket pocket and tossed it to him. "Ready, Buck?"

"Yeah." Nehlson stared at Max a moment. "If we pick up anything, I'll call you, Keene. Keep remembering this: you can't do her any good right now—and you might do her a lot of harm. Don't force him. It might trigger some more hell. Let him cool off. When he starts relaxing, that's when we jump."

Max gripped his gun. "I'm going to do more than jump, Nehlson."

"That's okay with me. In the meantime, go home—and wait."

"I suppose you're right," Max admitted reluctantly.

"I know I am."

"Okay, I'll go home."

Max went home. He dreamed about a huge green snake that glided caressingly about the slim curves of a girl with coppery-red hair who smiled sweetly and did a calypso song and dance while the snake became gradually smaller and smaller and finally disappeared completely, leaving a naked, white, tooth-torn body before his horrified eyes...

CHAPTER FOURTEEN

MAX AWOKE feeling as though he had been dogtrotting around an endless track all night. His arm ached and his head throbbed and he felt as spineless as a hammock. He forced himself up, stared at his watch. Eight-fifteen. The damned phone hadn't rung. He glared at the instrument, got to his feet, went to it. The receiver wasn't on crooked and there was a dial tone. He spun the dial irritably, picking out the number of the answering service. A girl's voice gave him a cheery good-morning and the uncheerful information that no one had called. He hung up feeling more frustrated than ever.

He bathed and dressed slowly, hoping the phone would ring. It didn't. At 8:45 he called Jim Barone and told him everything was under control. The lawyer was in his usual rush, so Max hung up, smoked a cigarette, checked his gun, smoked another cigarette. At 9.10 he went out, bought the *Tribune* and *Sun-Times,* and read them while eating breakfast. There was nothing except the usual political claptrap in the papers and Max ate with the uncomfortable feeling that the egg's yellow eyes were staring reproachfully around at the walls of his stomach. Before leaving the restaurant, he checked with the answering service again. Still no calls. Impatience had been gnawing at him, but he began to feel abject and helpless like a cow waiting to be milked.

More for the sake of having something to do than because the arm was bothering him, he drove to St. Joseph's hospital and had the bandages changed. Then he drove to his office. The mail had been delivered and several second-class envelopes and first-class bills lay on the floor inside the door.

Max picked them up and flung them unopened onto his desk. He called the answering service again. The girl's voice, more harassed than cheery now, reported no calls. Max cursed softly. Do nothing, Nehlson had said. *Nothing.* The word began to drum through his brain, rising to such a savage beat that he felt he had to do something—anything—or go quietly crazy.

He was standing at the window, staring down at the sun-drenched street and clenching and unclenching his hands nervously, when he remembered Tom Ames' message. He searched for the number and dialed it rapidly, praying that Ames had picked up a clue that would give him something to work on.

He was doomed to disappointment. Ames had had a girl go through the store's sales checks. The sale of the blue bra had, with only minor difficulty, been traced to one of the regular clerks' salesbook. The slip had not been written in the clerk's normal handwriting, however, so Ames had gone to the trouble of getting specimens of the handwriting of every male employee who had been on the floor at that time. Comparing the handwriting had been a laborious job—but it had paid off. The sale had been handled by an assistant buyer named Claude Farrell, who was 46 years old, had been with the store twelve years, was married for the second time, and had three kids. Farrell's record was excellent. He was considered energetic, dependable, imaginative, and ambitious. When the present buyer retired. Farrell would move into his job.

It was the story of Toliver all over again, and, feeling as though another hole had been jabbed into the precarious raft of hope on which he floated, Max asked Ames to see that a dependable earie was put on Farrell and to let him know if Farrell was seen in contact with anyone who might be a feeler. Ames said he would, absolutely without fail—and hung up.

The conversation with Ames reminded Max of Samuel Toliver, whom he had consigned to the somewhat dubious care of Red and Julie. The ghee had probably had a rough night. Red was handy with a deck of cards and had doubtless relieved Toliver of his loose cash; and what Red hadn't stolen, the girl had probably tried to earn by supplying a glimpse of his second childhood. Max grinned faintly, imagining the clerkish guy trying to evade Julie's determined charms, and decided to walk over to the Harp and bail him out.

Neither Red nor Julie were in the joint when Max got there, so he went upstairs. The room was locked. He rapped loudly and heard the creaky protest of rusty springs. Julie, looking bleary around the edges, opened the door. She wore a sleazy pink rayon nightgown beneath which everything except her name and address was visible. Toliver was stretched on the bed, naked as a jaybird, and appeared to be asleep.

"Jees, what time is it?" Julie groaned. She stretched her arms and fell back onto the bed beside Toliver. He wriggled close to her without opening his eyes and flung an arm across her hip. "Go on, beat it," she muttered. She pushed his hand away.

"How are you making out?" Max asked.

"I'm not," the girl said. She groaned again. "He and Red played gin most of the night, and Red won some dough, so he went out to get drunk," She nudged Toliver with her elbow. "This guy thinks he's a rabbit. Hey, wake up, lover, rise and shine!" Toliver made smacking sounds with his lips and inched his scrawny body toward her. "Oh, no, you don't." She elbowed him sharply. "The party's over. Come on, wake up!"

Toliver rolled away, muttering sleepily. She kicked at his legs, then swung and cracked him sharply across the butt. Protesting groggily, he opened his eyes. When he saw Max, he searched frantically for the rumpled sheet and tried to cover himself with it.

"Where did Red put his clothes?" Max asked.

"Down the hall, I guess." She eyed him a moment, then sat up and turned until her assets were exhibited at their best angle. "Want me to get them, Maxie?"

"Yeah. It's time he got out of here."

"You can say that again," She got up, jerked the door open, and pattered out into the hall.

"Get up, Toliver," Max ordered. "You're going home."

"Who wants to go home?" Toliver mumbled. "My wife's going to kill me."

Max smirked. "Tell her you sat up with a sick friend."

"You don't know my wife."

"No, but I know your friend."

Julie returned with an armful of clothes and tossed them on a chair. She pulled the nightgown over her head, wandered around looking for her bra and garter belt, and began dressing. Toliver stared at her like a man seeing the entire record of his horrid past flash before his eyes, then he threw his bony legs over the edge of the bed and clutched at his clothes. He dressed hurriedly and clumsily, as though painfully aware of the girl and anxious to get out of her sight. Max watched him sourly. Besides being an old fool, the guy was a jerk. When he finished dressing, he looked as though he had slept in his clothes—and acted like it, too.

"Thanks, Julie," Max said. He gestured Toliver toward the door.

She was shrugging her hips into a tight skirt. "Come and see me, Maxie, when you've got lots of time." She flashed him an arch look.

"Sure, kiddo. Saturday afternoon, maybe."

He closed the door. On the way downstairs, Toliver asked, "What about my job?"

"What about it?"

"You going to tell the store about—" Toliver licked at his lips, "—about this?"

"Don't you think I should?"

"Hell, you'd have done the same thing, wouldn't you? I was in a jam and had to get out of it, didn't I? I only did what any guy would do. That three grand Eddie said I owed—I probably didn't owe him a tenth of it! But they got me in the middle. And it isn't as though the store can't afford it. They didn't even miss anything, did they? It's what they call a calculated hazard. They *figure* on losing some merchandise!" Toliver sounded as though the argument had been simmering around within him for a long time.

"Nobody's made you a thief," Max said. "You did that, yourself."

"I didn't actually do any *stealing,*" Toliver said plaintively. "It was weeks—months—before I knew what was going on! That's the honest truth. But by then they had me hooked. Like dope, it was! Now that you know what's been going on, you'll break up the racket and they'll have to leave me alone. I won't have to ste—I mean, I won't have to tell them things anymore! See what I mean? I'm a good shopper. It'd cost the store a lot of money to teach another man to handle my job. You'd be giving us both a break. If you get me fired, what'll my wife and kids do? The store will blackball me and—"

They had reached the street, and the whining, twisting lies of the man was making him sick to his stomach. "Beat it," Max said harshly, pulling away from Toliver's clutching fingers. "Beat it before I throw you in the gutter where you belong..."

"Honest, I swear I—"

Max jerked away and balled his fist. Toliver saw the look on his face and cringed away. "Beat it the hell out of my sight," Max warned. "I'd rather associate with an honest whore like Julie than be touched by a rotten, lying, no-good punk of a thief like you."

Toliver turned and fled.

Max watched him until he turned the corner. Toliver had given him an idea. Max went into the drugstore on the corner, bought a pack of cigarettes, and consulted the telephone directory. Solly Franks was listed under Theatrical Agents and his office was in the Woods Building, which was on Randolph Street. Max got his car and headed for the Loop.

The glass door of the agent's office said simply, *Solly Franks. Walk In.* Max walked in. The outer office contained four walls plastered with hundreds of theatrical photos, a double row of chairs holding a dozen or more male and female show-types with hopeful smiles and bleak eyes, a wooden railing, and a sour-pussed old hen behind a desk. Max approached the old hen and said, "Tell Solly that Max Keene wants to see him."

"Max Keene?" She glanced at him and then her eyes wandered past his shoulder toward a photo-plastered wall as though trying to match him to one of the glossy, saccharine-smiling prints. "Is he expecting you?"

"No."

"Well...I don't know." She nodded toward the rows of chairs. "Will you have a chair, Mr. Keene? I'll ask Mr. Franks when he can see you."

"Don't ask him anything," Max said. "Tell him I'm here."

"Of course." With a resigned air, she did things with a phone on her desk. "There's a Max Keene here to see you, Mr. Franks." She held the receiver away from her ear a little as Solly Franks' screech rattled clearly out of the bakelite, "So tell him to sit down, for the love of—ain't I busy?" She dropped the phone as though it had snapped at her. "Mr. Franks will be busy for a while," she began mechanically. "Please have a cha—"

Max pushed back the gate and strode through. He twisted the knob of a door that bore the warning "Private," and, ignoring the old hen's frightened cackle behind him, kicked it open. In the agent's sanctum, a half-naked buxom brunette with the build and the long-lashed glance of a Jersey cow was swaying her arms gracefully and attempting a sort of low-slung bump and grind before a desk. Solly Franks lounged behind the desk in a swivel chair, his feet propped on a wastebasket and his eyes propped on the juiciest portion of the girl's anatomy. When the door banged open, Franks kicked the wastebasket over and shrieked, "Get the hell out! I'm busy!"

"Get rid of the chick," Max snapped.

"Wait your turn, buddy!" the agent shrieked, his voice jetting toward the treble. He was a little guy, nearly bald, with a spectacled face which had an unfinished look, but there was nothing unfinished about his gestures—he knew all of them. The girl, startled in the middle of a low bump, froze in an awkward position. "Get out, get out, *get out!*" Franks screamed, pounding his desk for sound effects.

"He means you," Max told the girl. "Wait outside, kiddo."

"Not her, *you,* you dumb sonuvabitch! Who do—"

The little agent was waving his arms and gesturing frenziedly. Max planted the palm of one hand against his tartan vest and shoved. Franks, gasping incoherently, stumbled back and landed in his swivel chair; the chair coasted back on squeaky wheels and crashed against the wall. The crash sent the girl leaping toward her clothes. She fled into the outer office. Max banged the door shut.

"The police!" Franks cried. "Get out, you crazy bastard, I'm calling the police...!"

"Better not," Max advised. He propped a hip on the corner of the agent's desk.

"If you're starving, I don't care!" Franks spat vehemently. "I can't use you. So go. You're wasting my time! I got talent waiting—"

"I'm a private detective," Max said.

"Ha, a Jack Webb type!" The agent snorted derisively. "Television I don't handle."

"I'm interested in Gwen Collyer."

"Gwen Collyer! Who's Gwen Collyer? I ain't even heard of her!"

"Little Harry gave her a try-out yesterday. You told him to kick her out."

A wary note crept into the agent's voice, "A redhead?"

"That's the one."

"Look, Mister Big Shot Private Eye..." The agent stabbed a finger at his desk like a general indicating a field maneuver to a very stupid captain. "...I don't care how many friends you got or what you promised the girl or how much dough you got to spend, nobody's pressuring Solly Franks! The girl's out, period. Her act's no good. Now beat it."

"Who told you to nix her?"

"Who told me? Are you crazy? I saw her. Like a clubfoot she dances! No talent, no talent at all—"

"The customers liked her."

"The customers!" Franks blew rudely through his lips.

"A pretty face, a can that wriggles—maybe two days, maybe three days she'd last. For my shows she's no good. Maybe some other agent—who knows?" He shrugged.

"What if she got herself a snake, like Sally Breeze?"

"Sally's got a real act, a real *artiste*—" Franks seemed to remember something. "What'd you say the name was? Max who?"

"Keene."

There was a different note in Franks' voice. "What's your connection with Sally?"

"Sally had a tough time getting a job. You got her in at the Tropic."

"Mr. Keene," A plastic-like film slid over the agent's eyes. "I'm an agent. When I place an act, I get a slice of it. It don't pay me to waste time on bum acts. Sally's act had moxie. I saw a chance to fit her in at the Tropic Isle and I made a couple of bucks doing it. Strictly business, understand? If this girl, this redhead, had a socko act like Sally's, I'd grab her. I'd sign her up, put her in a good spot—and make a buck. I'd be crazy if I didn't."

"You aren't crazy," Max admitted, "but you aren't real smart, either. You couldn't see Sally's act until somebody pressured you—and they pressured you until you went along with the deal."

"Nobody pressures Solly Franks!" The agent's face started to get red again. "Nobody tells—"

"Somebody did," Max insisted.

"Nobody! Positively nobody! You're a crazy, lying—" His voice started to leap and skip shrilly.

"You've been doing it for other girls besides Sally," Max said quietly. "You must have gotten yourself jammed up. What'd you do? Fall for one of these torso twisters?"

"Get out!" The phrase seemed to be Franks' favorites litany. "Get out! Nobody pressures me. You can't come, here and—"

"Listen, Solly." Max kept his voice level. "I'm not trying to make trouble for you. Sally was murdered. So was another girl. And Gwen Collyer, the girl you nixed last night, has been snatched. When things blow up, you're going to be in the middle. You'll be publicized as a killer's pawn, an agent who took orders to save his own skin. My hand isn't out. All I want is information—and I'm going to get it, or else."

"What would I know about killers?" Franks asks wildly. "I'm an agent. I handle talent. I'm—"

"Cut it off, Solly. I'm not an agent but I know an act when I see one—and yours stinks. Look—you handle mostly shows for dine-and-drink joints. They're mostly syndicate-controlled, so—"

"Syndicate!" Franks groaned. "What's a syndicate? Don't tell—"

"Okay, you never heard of the syndicate—but maybe you've heard of Jim Barone?"

"Barone?" Franks narrowed his eyes. "Sure. Barone's a springer."

"Good. Get him on the phone. His number is in the book."

Franks stiffened a little and stared at the phone as though it might leap at him. "Why?" he demanded. "Why should I call Barone?"

"Because it'll save us both a hell of a lot of time," Max told him. "Barone represents the syndicate. You get most of your business from syndicate-controlled joints. It won't cost you anything to talk to Barone, and it might cost you plenty if you don't."

Franks took off his spectacles, polished them nervously, and replaced them on his nose. "What's your connection with Barone?" he asked.

"Ask him."

The agent considered a moment, then reluctantly reached for the phone directory and looked up Barone's; number. He scribbled it on a pad, hesitated, then pulled the phone toward him. He plucked out the number irritably as though every click of the dial was costing him money. Max waited until the connection was made, then, he plucked the receiver from Franks' fingers.

"Jim? This is Max. I'm in the office of a talent peddler named Solly Franks. He's giving me the run-around. Square me with him, will you?" Max handed the receiver back to Franks.

"Barone?" the agent asked. "This is Solly Franks." His eyes became quiet and something seemed to die in them as he listened. "Yeah... Well, I thought I better check," the agent mumbled. "Sure... Well, I'm just trying to do a job, Barone... Okay... Of course... Just a minute." He handed the receiver to Max and slumped down in his chair.

Max said, "Yeah, Jim."

"I told him you were a screwy bastard but could be trusted," Barone's mild voice said. "What's going on?"

"I think I'm close to an answer," Max said, watching the agent. "Another girl got killed yesterday and last night Gwen Collyer was snatched. I'll tell you about it later Jim."

"Keep my clients out of this, Max," Barone warned.

"Natch." Max replaced the receiver, then said, "How about it, Solly? Who's got their hooks into you?"

CHAPTER FIFTEEN

"I WISH I knew!" the agent muttered. He stared somberly at the wall as though seeing his obituary written there. "I've been in this business thirty-seven years. Started handling hoofers back during vaudeville. I never cheated anybody, always supplied the best talent, tried to build good acts, never handed anybody a bum show if I could help it—until a year ago."

"That's when it started?" Max asked.

"Yeah." Solly Franks took off his spectacles and rubbed his eyes. "I'm trusting you because Jim Barone says I should. This is just between us, understand? Absolutely one hundred percent confidential."

"Of course." Max nodded.

"I handle lots of dames. Naturally. I get all kinds. Every girl who can play a piano or won a dance contest or thinks she can sing, right away they leave home and come to Chicago to make money. They hang around the joints, they bother the managers, they talk to their friends. Eventually they learn about agents and they come to Solly Franks thinking they're giving me and the business a break. Good lord, you should see the pigs that think they should be paid to sing! No class, no real talent, nothing! So I'm on the spot, see? I want to tell them the truth, but it's hard. A girl thinks she can sing—well, maybe she can. But she's been doing the singing for her friends maybe a couple of times a week, she's got teeth like a horse, she's built like an army sergeant, and all she's got for scenery is a gown she used to wear to parties in Waterloo, Iowa. What can I do? I can't sell her. I can't even tell her the truth. In fact, the truth is no good. They never believe it anyway. So usually I take the easy out and say things are tough, leave your name and telephone, I'll call you. I'm hoping she'll start to starve and get smart and go home where she belongs. I'm running a business, so what else can I do?"

"Not much," Max agreed.

"It's obvious. But some of these girls aren't pigs. Some are young, pretty; they got socko equipment. I spot it right away, naturally. But ninety percent of the time something's wrong. I spot a girl with the figure for stripping, either she thinks she's a concert violinist or she's a strict Baptist. I get a girl I think has got the looks for peddling sexy songs, she wants to do ballet dancing or be a dramatic actress. Most of the time, they got the looks and no talent. So again I'm on the spot, but this time it's a big temptation. Suppose I get a girl who looks like Arlene Dahl—and plays the piano about as good? What should I do? As talent, she stinks. I can't sell her even for nothing. But I got red blood and she looks like a good sport and she wants to play the piano real bad." The agent shrugged. "A guy in my business, he gets so he can spot them. I know she's strictly a pushover. Five will get you eight that she's read about the entertainment racket, she's heard about girls who became stars by being screen-tested on their backs—and I'm an agent, ain't I? All I got to do is make with some promises and she's right there waiting when I'm ready to drop the anchor. Hell, when I was younger, I'd see a doll like that and I couldn't sleep until she'd done me some good—and I'm not talking about getting myself a slice of her salary. It was there, she was asking for it, so why shouldn't I help myself? Sometimes I'd get big-hearted and put her in a show for a few nights. That got me off the hook. Sometimes a manager would see her and she'd hit him just right. Again, I was off the hook. Usually she'd get smart and snag a sucker and get married. I didn't give a damn, just so I got on and off okay, see, so it was always a temptation. Like somebody once said, the best way of getting rid of a temptation is by giving in to it. Until about three years ago I used to give in plenty."

"What happened three years ago?"

"A doll came in, wanted me to get her a spot pounding the ivories." Franks smiled wryly. "I took one look at her and nearly climbed over my desk. Young, cute smile, pretty golden hair—and a strictly terrific figure. I listened to her play. She went over the keys like she had mitts on. With me, the music she played was for borscht, but the rest of the stuff she had was socko. I gave her a line. Hell, I should have figured something was wrong because she started flopping before I even pushed hard. But I only had my mind on the usual thing and, like most guys, I didn't know what was wrong until too late. Anyway, the cops walked in on us. The vice squad. The kid was jailbait, she'd run away from home, her father was a big shot in the Elks, and he was going to blow his top. When the cops started ticking out the facts, I nearly fainted. It was the end, I figured. I was on my way to jail, my business was shot to hell—and my wife and kids would hate me forever. Luckily, a friend of mine talked to a couple of parties and got in a fix for me."

"You thought," Max said cynically.

"No, the fix was straight. They held me a few hours, then let me go. It cost me five grand, but it was worth it. I don't know what kind of a story they gave the girl, but she kept her mouth shut and I never heard any more about it—until about a year ago."

"Who were the cops?"

"I don't even remember their names. I heard later my mistake had been in going to this particular hotel. The clerk had a deal on with the cops, and when he saw me and the girl going up to her room together, he tipped them and they came up. Maybe he got a cut of the five grand. Maybe the two

cops cut it up and he got his some other way. I was out—
and that's all that mattered."

"Did you check on the girl?"

"Believe me, Mr. Keene, just thinking about her made me
sick. I paid the dough and I've been keeping my nose pretty
clean ever since. Look but don't touch, that's my motto now.
Understand?"

"They shook you for five grand," Max said slowly. "It was
a sucker trap, not that you didn't deserve to get your neck
caught in it. When did they try for the bite?"

"About a year ago. I thought it was dead. Hell, I'd nearly
forgotten about it. Then I got a letter."

"What kind of a letter?"

"An envelope with a note and a picture. I took one look
at the picture and nearly swallowed my teeth. It showed me
and the girl and there wasn't any doubt about what was going
on. Everything was in it, even a calendar on the wall to show
what month and year it was. I wanted to shoot myself. Five
grand—and they still had a picture! All they had to do was
show it to the girl's old man and I'd be—"

"What did the note say?" Max interrupted.

"It told me to be in my office the next morning at ten
o'clock. That's all. Just be in my office! I didn't know what
to expect. I sat right here the next morning, waiting for them
to come and get me, waiting to find out what it was going to
cost me, but all I got was a phone call."

"From who?"

"A man. That's all I know. He sounded kind of screwy,
like he had a nickel between his teeth, see, and he didn't talk
much, just enough to tell me that I had to play ball—or else.
He had everything, he said, some more pictures and copies of
the records and everything. He was going to shut up as long
as I did like he told me, and what I had to do was find spots
for some girls he was going to send me."

"Look, Solly. This guy who called you. Could it have been one of the cops, do you think?"

"It could be a cop, a clerk, anybody. What difference does it make?" Franks shrugged hopelessly. "I can't kill him. I don't even know where he is. But I still got my business and my wife and my kids. I'm not as young as I used to be and those are the things that count now. He calls me two-three times a month, always for a job for Some girl. Sometimes they work out fine. Like Sally Breeze. I got no complaints on her. But some of the others?" He chuckled. "Sometimes I feel like locking the door. I get screams from my customers, but what can I do?"

"What happened last night, Solly?"

"You mean about the redhead?"

"Yeah."

"Ain't it obvious? Harry asked me to come out and have a look at her. He thought she was hot stuff, something new, something the customers would go for. Harry's a nice guy, so I went; besides business is business. I walk in and the bartender's got a number for me to call. When I can it, this guy says to kick her out fast." The agent spread his hands helplessly. "The act wasn't bad, but it's me or her, so I don't argue."

"Remember the number?"

"I still got it." Franks dug a finger into a pocket of the tartan vest. He found a scrap of paper, adjusted his spectacles, peered at it. "Sure, this is it. You can ask the bartender."

Max took the scrap of paper. The number was the same as the one Little Harry had said that Mabel Tangier had left for him to call. Max tossed it onto the desk. "This guy you talked to," Max asked, "did he sound like a nance?"

"No. Screwy, but not like that." Franks shook his head positively.

"The clerk at the hotel. What'd he look like?"

"Tall, slender, a dancer type."

"Young or old."

"Thirty, maybe thirty-five."

Max grunted. "Dark hair?"

"I should remember after three years? I was with the girl. I hardly looked at him."

"How about the two cops? You looked at them, didn't you?"

"Sure, but a cop is a cop. They were both big guys, not so young, in plainclothes. I looked at their guns and thought about how it would look in the papers and got too sick to see much. You think I'd try to remember them? I wanted to forget the whole thing, as soon as possible!"

"How about your friend? Do you think he'd remember?"

"He didn't talk to them."

"How'd he work the fix, then?"

"He owned a joint and had connections through the syndicate."

"Do you think you'd recognize either of those cops if you saw them again?"

The agent's shrug indicated disinterest. "Probably not."

"You've never seen either of them since?"

"No."

"But you make the rounds of the joints regularly. You must run into a lot of the vice cops."

"Believe me, Mr. Keene, when I see a cop, I don't put my arms around him."

"Have you gotten any dough out of this arrangement?"

"The usual ten percent slice."

"Nothing extra?"

"Are you crazy?" Franks replaced his spectacles and stared at Max as though Max had suddenly sprouted three heads.

"If he tells me to forget the commission, I forget it. What choice have I?"

Max realized that he was going around in circles and grabbing at empty air, but he asked, "Do you know where the girl is now?"

"No." Franks was emphatic. "I should drop dead if I ever saw her again!"

"Have you got a photo of her?"

"I burned it."

"Well, what was her name?"

"Please, Mr. Keene." Franks looked ill. "Digging all this up isn't necessary, is it?"

"Maybe not," Max admitted. "I wish to hell you could remember those cops. Did you hear their names?"

"No. If I did, I don't remember."

Max sighed. "Well, that's it, then, I guess. Thanks, Solly. If we nab him, I'll see that you're protected," Max got up. "Want me to send the bump artist back in?"

"Girls!" Franks muttered. He was staring at his desk as though seeing the face of a deadly enemy. "A man my age should look at girls! Better I should be a carpenter, maybe. Tell them all to go home. Tell them I'm sick."

Max closed the door and gave the message to the old hen. She clucked at him, looked frightened, and grabbed at the phone as though for anchorage. The chairs were still filled with hopeful smiles and bleak eyes. Max glanced at them as he walked to the door. He wondered if any of them realized how small a chance they had.

And then he thought about Sally Breeze.

And Gwen.

CHAPTER SIXTEEN

THE ANSWERING service had recorded three calls: Sergeant Halloran had called at 10:18 and wanted Mr. Keene to phone him at police headquarters; Sergeant Nehlson had called twice, at 10:35 and again at 11:30, and also wanted to be contacted at police headquarters. Max called Nehlson first. It took a while for the police switchboard to locate him.

"Max Keene, sergeant. Any news?" Max held his breath.

"Not yet." Nehlson sounded worried. "Something occurred to me, Keene. You know what happened to Sally Breeze's snake?"

"No."

"It's missing. Danny Green said you'd been asking about it."

"You know everything I do, then. Any ideas?"

"The obvious ones. I don't like the idea of that snake floating around. A stranger wouldn't have a chance. I've checked with all the vets. They all told me the same thing.

Animals and birds they'd pick up and treat, but snakes they don't mess around with. I called the Brookfield and Lincoln Park zoos, too; nobody has given them any big snakes lately."

"Damn..." Max shuddered.

"In spades," Nehlson said. "Get any calls?"

"No."

Nehlson was silent a moment. "That's damned funny."

"You've checked the morgue?"

"She's not there." Nehlson was silent again, then he said, "I don't get it. She's no use to them except as a hammer. They should have started pounding by now."

"If they have, I haven't heard it."

"Funny. Where were you digging all morning?"

"I talked to Solly Franks," Max said casually. "Know him?"

"Sure." There was no hesitation in Nehlson's reply. "He handles the shows in most of the joints. Kind of soft for girls. Likes them fresh from the farm. What about him?"

"You mean he still likes them?"

"Why not? He isn't dead, is he?" Nehlson laughed.

"No, but he got in a jam about three years ago. Somebody from Vice picked him up and gave him a hard time. Know anything about it?"

"It's news to me. Guess it happened while I was still on Robbery. Want me to get the record on it?"

"I doubt if there is a record. A pal of his made a motion to fix." Without changing his tone, Max added, "You can do me a favor, though."

"Providing it doesn't cost me dough."

"I need the address that goes with this number." Max read the phone number to him.

Nehlson repeated it, then said, "It'll take a few minutes. I'll call you back."

"Fine." Max broke the connection, dialed again, and asked for Sergeant Halloran in Homicide. Halloran's hello sounded tired and anti-social. "Max Keene, sergeant. I hear you called me."

"Yeah," Halloran snapped grumpily. "What was the idea of ducking out yesterday?"

"You didn't want me to hang around, did you?"

"Hell, you're a suspect, Keene, in case you don't know it!"

"Like hell. For once I've got an alibi."

"Who?"

"Not who, *what,*" Max corrected. "Ever hear of a one-armed guy strangling a strong woman?"

"Hell, that's no alibi!" Halloran's snort rattled the receiver. "You could have done it *before* you got shot."

"Haven't they established a time of death?"

"It happened between three-thirty and four a.m. wise guy, which includes you in."

"At 3:30 I was flopping on one wing. You must be damned hard up for suspects."

"I am." Halloran's voice sounded tired again. "Got any ideas, shamus?"

"A couple." Max picked up a pencil on his desk and began doodling a rooster with a peacock-like tail.

"For instance." Halloran sounded interested.

"Well, Sally got her job through Solly Franks, the agent," Max said. He drew sharp claws on the rooster. "About three years ago a couple of cops in Vice picked him up and gave him a hard time. Know anything about it?"

"I heard something about it," Halloran admitted. He sounded puzzled. "He was caught messing with some kid, wasn't he? What'd he get, a suspended sentence?"

"Somebody fixed it. You were assigned to Vice then, weren't you, Halloran?"

"So what?"

"Who were the cops?" Max began drawing a pyramid of eggs near the rooster.

"Hell, I don't know. Want me to check?"

"I doubt if there's anything to check. When the fix went in, they probably cleaned the record. Would anybody have a roster of the vice detail three years back?"

There was a moment of silence, then Halloran said, "Commissioner's office might. You'd have to explain why you wanted it, though."

"The hell with it." Max sketched in a tree and a waning moon. "How about doing me a favor, Halloran? I need an address to go with a number I picked up," He read the number to him.

Halloran repeated the number and said, "Hang on, Keene." The line hummed emptily for sixty seconds, then the receiver rattled and Halloran's voice quoted Mabel Tangier's address on Arlington Place.

"Thanks, Halloran." Max printed it in large capitals beneath the rooster. "Who's it listed for?"

"Robert Downing. This got anything to do with the killing, Keene?"

"I doubt it," Max told him. "Somebody called and left it and I haven't been able to get an answer. What about the Parreo thing?"

"Nothing new."

"Nothing on Sally, either?"

"No."

"Want me to come down?"

"I'll let you know." Halloran's voice was suddenly edged as though the conversation was annoying him. "Don't leave town without letting me know, shamus." He hung up abruptly.

Max put down the receiver and began drawing another rooster on a second sheet of paper. This one was a scrawny bird, flat chested and nearly featherless. With infinite care, he then drew a huge coiling snake behind the rooster. He ornamented the snake with a skin diamond like an Indian blanket and added tiers of rattlers to its tail. He was working on a venom-spewing mouth that bristled with fangs when the phone rang. Max tossed the pencil aside and snatched up the receiver.

It was Sergeant Nehlson. "I had some trouble getting it," Nehlson explained. "It's an unlisted private line." He quoted the same address Halloran had and added, "The subscriber is a Robert Downing. What's your angle, Keene? That address must be almost across the street from where Sally Breeze lived."

"That's right," Max said. He sketched a pair of improbable horns on the snake.

"Who is this Downing? You know him?" Nehlson demanded.

"I don't know," Max said. "Little Harry said somebody wanted me to call it."

"Oh. Well, maybe it's none of my business." Nehlson switched subjects. "About that snake, Keene. If you get any ideas, call me. I'm kind of bothered."

"Sure, sergeant. Where'll you be?"

"Leave word here. I'll check with the switchboard."

After hanging up Max sat a moment, smoking a cigarette. Then he began adding an ornamental border to the snake sketch. The border was almost completed when he suddenly ripped the paper to pieces and flung them violently from him.

He said softly, "You rotten cop bastard..."

Arlington Place is a comparatively quiet residential street and in the early afternoon it is virtually deserted. The men are still at their stores, earning the large rent that goes with their small apartments, the housewives are resting from their morning expeditions to the A. & P , the unmarried girls are in Loop offices, pounding their typewriters and trying to wangle dinner dates, and the kept women are lazily eating brunch and beginning to worry about the cocktail fracas ahead. Since the post office ceased making afternoon deliveries, the only persons seen on Arlington Place in the early afternoon are delivery boys or repairmen, who are uncooperative individuals at best.

Max, clad in grease-spattered tan coveralls and carrying a battered metal tool case, strolled unnoticed along the street. When he reached Mabel Tangier's building, he set the case on the sidewalk for a moment and pretended to consult a notebook that he took from a pocket. His eyes studied the building covertly. The building appeared to be as deserted as the street. Max put the notebook back into his pocket, picked up the case, and went around to the rear of the building. The yard was bright with flowers but Max gave them scant attention. The gate was unlocked. No one was puttering in the yard. A zigzag of steep wooden stairs led to the third floor. No one was visible on any of the porches. Whistling casually, Max opened the gate and started up the wooden stairs.

There was a garbage can and an old canvas-covered cot on the third-floor porch. There was also a door and three windows. All three of the windows were covered with a wide-mesh grill. The aluminum screen-door was hooked inside and the inner door looked strong enough to resist an elephant. Max set down the tool case and pressed the button beside the door. A shrill buzzer rang somewhere within the apartment. Max flexed his wounded arm gently—and waited.

There was no response.

Max slit the aluminum screening with a knife, poked a finger through, and released the hook. Opening the door, he knelt and studied the lock. It was a standard tumbler lock, not much of an obstacle by itself, but, when he tested the door by applying pressure at various points, it resisted him in a way which suggested that there was probably an inside bolt. He closed the screen-door gently and strolled to the windows. All three shades were drawn. Max grasped the wide-mesh grill and tested it. It was strong, but, like most so-called burglarproof inventions, was more of a hindrance than an absolute deterrent. There were two steel lugs on each side of the grill. The lugs were screwed to the inside of the window frame, holding the grill solidly in place. To an amateur, the screws might be inaccessible, but Max had borrowed a set of second-story specials from an expert at the business. The long flexible-shaft screwdriver went through the mesh and found the screw-head. Elbow grease and a few grunts loosened the screws, and, one by one, they fell to the porch. Max slipped the screwdriver into his pocket and tugged at the grill. It left the window frame as willingly as a tired lover.

Max rested for a minute by smoking a cigarette and surveying the neighboring buildings. In most of the buildings, window shades were drawn and venetian blinds were closed against the hot slanting rays of the August sun. Down the block, a woman came out, slammed garbage into a can, and returned to her kitchen. Max snapped his cigarette away and got a wide roll of plastic tape from the tool chest. He cut off a six-inch strip of the sticky black tape and pressed it onto the glass above the lock. Two sharp blows with a wooden mallet shattered the glass almost silently, and, by simply peeling the glass fragments away, the lock became accessible. Max loosened it and slid the window upward. He touched his pocket to make certain his gun was handy, then he pushed the shade aside and swung his head and shoulders into the room beyond.

It was a small, cheaply furnished bedroom, containing a barracks—neat cot, a chair, a reading lamp, a rack of rather gaudy neckties, and a table laden with garish true-crime magazines. Max gave the room a swift glance, listened intently for a moment, then eased himself in, closed the window and adjusted the shade. Walking quietly, he went to the door of the room and inched it open. The apartment was as silent as a dancehall on Monday morning.

His stomach relaxed a little as he stepped into the kitchen. There was the usual culinary equipment, a stack of used cups on the sink, and a profusion of scattered crumbs on a dish-cluttered table. A few of the crumbs moved uncertainly, then fled toward a crack in the wall as Max crossed toward the door. He unlocked and unbolted the door, leaving it open an inch to facilitate flight—if and when necessary. Then, taking the gun from his pocket, he headed for a hall that obviously led to the rest of the apartment.

He found her in the third bedroom.

She lay immobile across the rumpled sheet of an old-fashioned four-poster bed with her face buried in the loose mass of reddish hair like a pallid flower engulfed in a puddle of molten copper. Stifling the cry that rose in his throat, Max ran to her. Her outflung arms were bound by rough ropes to the head-posts of the bed. Her eyes were closed, and, in the pale light of the room, her face seemed bloodless.

He brushed a strand of hair away from her forehead.

"Gwen!" he called softly. *"Gwen!"*

She didn't move. Fear plucked at him, but he pushed it away. She couldn't be dead. She couldn't! The front of her blouse was torn, as though ripped away by an angry hand. Forcing himself to move deliberately, Max laid the gun on the bed and slid his hand through the tear until his palm was resting against her chest. The skin was warm and moist, and, after what seemed an eternity, he felt her lungs slowly expand and then contract. He smiled faintly in relief and shifted his hand gently until it nestled between her breasts. He felt nothing for a long moment...then her heartbeat throbbed through his fingers—strong, deep, regular. She was doped—but she was alive! Suddenly overcome by a flood of emotion that he hadn't suspected, he bent and kissed her lips.

She moaned a little and tried to turn her head.

"You're all right, darling," Max murmured. "Everything's all right!"

He had freed one of her hands and was circling the bed to reach the knots that bound the other one when a heavy *thump* startled him. He froze—and waited. After a long interval, it came again. A hollow sort of reverberation followed the second *thump*. The sound seemed to come from behind a door on the other side of the room. Max tiptoed to the door and pressed an ear against it. The *thump* came again, clear and definite, like the heavy thud of a sand-filled sack swinging against heavy metal. Max opened the door a half-inch and glimpsed the white tile of a bathroom. The *thumping* became agitated and louder. Max eased the door back cautiously, thrust an arm in, and snapped on the light.

"What...the...hell!" he muttered.

A huge black snake was confined in the glass-doored bathnook. As Max stared at it, the python reared its head up, weaving it back and forth malevolently, then the snake slowly slithered across the tub, its glistening body undulating powerfully, and began to climb up the tile. It seemed to flow across the chrome faucet and water controls, reaching high toward the gleaming curved neck of the showerhead, and its ugly mouth opened and closed spasmodically as though already chewing at the metal. It lunged toward the showerhead suddenly—missed—and fell with a heavy *thump* into the empty tub.

Max shuddered and backed away from the door. Behind him, a voice taunted, "Pretty, isn't she, shamus?"

CHAPTER SEVENTEEN

"SO I WAS right," Max said softly.

Halloran's smile was thin and icy. "You got too smart, shamus. Sometimes it doesn't pay," Halloran gestured with his gun. "Hands on the wall and back two steps, before I get nervous, Keene."

Max obeyed. Halloran moved around behind him cautiously, slapped his pockets, chest and thighs, and removed the screwdriver. When Halloran stepped away, Max walked to the wall, lowered his arms, and forced himself not to look at Gwen. He had laid his revolver beside her, but Halloran hadn't been near the bed. Could she have shifted her skirt and covered it—or was it still in plain sight? Max stared at Halloran, willing his eyes away from the bed.

"Didn't even bring a rod, huh?" Halloran seemed amused. "I thought you private dicks didn't feel dressed unless you had at least one in your belt."

"Lead's too good for a crooked cop like you, Halloran."

"You want to know something?" The amusement in the big cop's voice tightened as though a vein of sincerity had become tangled in his vocal chords. "I wasn't always a crooked cop. I didn't want to be crooked. But *people* made me this way." His voice cracked a little. "Everybody snipes at cops! We're lazy, we're dumb, we're crooked, we always got our mitts out. To read the papers, you'd think all we did was drink beer and hand out parking tickets. How long you think a cop can take that? If we're to get the blame, why shouldn't we get the dough, too?"

"Pressuring young kids to do your dirty work is worse than taking handouts, Halloran," Max said.

"I never pressured a kid in my life! I—"

"How about the girl you caught Solly Franks with?"

"You think she was a kid?" Halloran laughed. "Hell, she was born a floozy and was doing tricks before she got out of grade school!"

"That isn't the way Solly tells it."

"Solly's a dumb jerk when it comes to girls. I'll admit she made it look good, but he was scared stiff and didn't even bother to check. I was a cop and she even convinced me. I figured we had him cold and I was in favor of throwing the book at him."

"You did have him cold. Solly admits it."

"Didn't I tell you he was dumb? The girl was sixteen, sure, but she was a tramp from the day she entered kindergarten. And like I told you, she started doing tricks while she was in grade school. If he'd checked, he'd have found out her parents were both drunks and didn't care if she dropped dead. The whole thing was strictly a set-up and the girl knew what she was doing from the word go."

"But you still took five grand of his dough."

"I didn't even see his dough! And I didn't know about the set-up until six or eight months later, after it had all blown over." Halloran scowled. "That's another thing. The average cop is supposed to be a rotten, crooked, lazy, fat, dumb punk—but what about the big boys? When a fix like Solly Franks' goes in, who gets it—the cop who handled the pinch? Like hell. Maybe the lieutenant gets a slice, maybe the captain takes a chunk, maybe the sergeant on the desk gets paid, maybe the state's attorney's boy gets a dip of the gravy—maybe even the mayor and the commissioner get in on the deal—and the cop gets a kick in the fanny. Solly paid five grand—and what do you think I got? I made the pinch and might shoot off my mouth, so I got shifted from Vice, where I could have made a few bucks, to Homicide where the only fixes the customers want are the Big Fix."

"I guess that's what you need, Halloran," Max said.

"Not yet." The cop moistened his lips.

"You've got the blood of two girls on your hands, Halloran."

"I've got news for you, Keene." Halloran showed his teeth in a hard smile. "Before the day is over, I'll be sitting pretty. You know what the papers are going to say? The headline's going to be: POLICE SERGEANT TRAPS TRIPLE KILLER. Pretty good, huh? I might even get a medal."

"There are too many holes in it, Halloran. You'll never make it hang together." Max tried to suppress the chill that nibbled at his spine. "And there are only two dead—Helen Parreo and Sally Breeze."

Halloran's teeth glinted. "Don't forget her." He jerked his head toward the bed. "You can walk through the pearly gates with her, hand in hand. And with marks on her just like the ones on Helen, the public will forget we couldn't pin the middle murder on you—they'll figure you killed Sally, all right, but managed to pull the wool over our eyes on that one. My guys won't push in too deep...us cops will be tickled to have found someone, anyone, to wash the case out of the books and show how good we are at catching sex fiends."

"You must be crazy, Halloran. Gwen isn't involved in any way..." Involuntarily, Max took a step toward the cop. "For pete's sake, at least—"

"Another step and I shoot," Halloran warned.

Max stopped. "Listen to me, Halloran. What has Gwen done? Why kill her? She doesn't even know—"

"I'm not so sure," the cop said. "I think she saw me with the Parreo kid a couple of times. Anyway, I'm not taking any chances. With you and her out of the way, I can liquidate the racket and take the stake I've made to South America without leaving any loose ends behind. Things were about ready to blow up anyway. Incidentally, how'd you spot me, shamus?"

"I didn't—until I talked to you on the phone this morning."

"What'd I say wrong?" Halloran frowned.

"You got that address a little bit too fast. I asked Nehlson to do the same favor and it took him a good ten minutes."

"You mean Sergeant Buck Nehlson?" Halloran grinned. "What a frying pan that poor dumb bastard's going to be on. The way things worked out, you'd think he was on my team!"

"He knows the whole story, Halloran."

"Nehlson can be dealt with. One thing about cops, dumb as they are, they know enough to stick together," Halloran nodded thoughtfully. "So I gave you the number too fast and right away you figured I didn't need to go to the trouble of looking it up. Well, everybody makes a few mistakes. It's how well they cover them up that counts, and I'm going to do a slick job of covering up. With you out of my hair—"

"Why did you kill Helen Parreo, Halloran?"

"She was like you, shamus—she got too smart for her britches." The cop's face sobered fleetingly. "Do you think I wanted to do it? No more than I want to kill you. I even took you out of her apartment, dumped you through the first door my skeletons would open. To get rid of your fingerprints, I managed to accidentally smash that glass and whiskey bottle. And after that dame screamed she'd seen you with Helen, I made no real try to pick you up. I didn't want you burning for something I did. Hell, I'm no killer. Any more than I'm a sex maniac. That was just a gag—something to give motive to a mysterious stranger. Why, if you hadn't kept poking around, nosing in on my girls and my business, I wouldn't be on your neck now. But you forced me...you wouldn't let well enough alone..."

"Like Helen?"

"Like Helen. She wasn't a bad kid, really. I met her at that dancing school where she used to work and I figured that as long as she had a husband in the background it'd be safe to play around with her. But she was determined to get her hooks into me and I found out she was divorcing her husband—and then she started pulling the old 'gotta' line. Said she'd been smelling around, like you, and had learned a thing or two about my racket—but hell, I don't gotta do anything...and I proved it."

"Sally was the one you wanted, then."

"Yeah, I had quite a fire going for her, not that it ever did me much good." A shadow flickered in Halloran's eyes. "I wish to hell I'd killed you that night! I guess I was too mad to shoot straight. This will make up for it, maybe. She's the only woman I ever really wanted—and you, you bastard, you had to take her. I was watching from in there—" Halloran tipped his head toward the front of the apartment—" and I saw you follow her upstairs. I looked right in and saw you drinking and grabbing for each other. And when you turned the lights out, I almost blasted at you through the window." Halloran's face was flushed with anger suddenly. "She was a bitch a lousy, snake-loving bitch. I should have cut her to pieces the way she cut my heart. Strangling was too good for her. Cheating with you, right in front of my eyes—"

Gwen moaned softly and moved her legs.

"The worst of it," Halloran said, "was that I gave you an alibi! What you told me in Sally's dressing room made me realize I'd have to get rid of you. I left instructions that Mabel should give you the phone number of the boss— meaning me—so I could lead you on into some trap. But I had no chance to tip Verne, and he just cut you off when you called. But I could have hung you with Sally's death—except I was so blind mad I put that alibi-bullet into you..."

Halloran shook his head and passed his left hand across his forehead. Max watched the gun. Though Halloran seemed shaken, the gun didn't waver.

"It left me no choice but to pick up this doll here," the cop said. "She's my chance to frame you, Max. And to get even with you for spoiling Sally for me—"

"Max—!" Gwen's eyes were open and she had lifted her head. "Max! Oh gosh, what are you doing here?" There was terror and concern and hopelessness in her voice.

"Be quiet, Gwen," Max said as steadily as he could. Everything's okay."

Halloran laughed harshly. "Listen to him. Everything's okay! Sure, it is, baby. You and your boy friend are going for a little walk together. Won't that be nice?"

"Walk?" Gwen looked pale and weak. She tried to raise herself, but the rope cut into her wrist and she fell back with a sob. "What does he mean Max?"

"He's going to kill us, darling." The endearment slipped out easily, and it sounded right. "He killed Helen Parreo and Sally Breeze—and we're next."

A fold of her skirt had fallen over the revolver but Max could glimpse its butt. Hope surged within him for an instant, then died. It was too far away. Even a lousy triggerman could blast his guts out before he got halfway there. But if he could distract Halloran long enough...if he could only tell her the gun was there...she might...she just might be able to get it and...Max closed his eyes a moment and thought, *Gwen, darling...under the skirt...there's a gun...you can reach it...try, darling, please try...it's our only hope.* But, when he opened his eyes she was smiling at him, a smile full of love—and death.

"Well, let's see," Halloran was saying, "we may as well get this over with. This will ruin my camp, but I guess it can't be avoided." His voice and his eyes were cold and calculating. "Stand nearer to the girl, shamus. I want it to look as though I came waltzing in and caught you m the act." He took a smaller revolver from his jacket. "Guess I may as well try for the medal. I'll make it look as though you went down shooting, Keene. You'll be a real fighting killer—" He stopped and frowned. "Hell, I forgot the damned snake. Let's see. First the redhead, with this," He gripped the smaller gun. "Then you, Keene." He moved his Police Special. "Then bang-bang at the door and wall to show you went down fighting. He shook the smaller gun again. "Then the snake. It hasn't eaten for two days and it hates strangers. The blood will excite it. It'll head straight for you, shamus, and I'll let it get a good grip, just enough so you'll remember Sally before you die—and then I'll give it a couple of bullets in the head," He nodded. "That'll make a terrific story. Keene you're going to be the darling of the front pages for at least a week." His lips twisted cynically. "Want to say a prayer?"

Max took a step toward the bed. "Let me kiss her goodbye, Halloran," he said hoarsely. "Okay?"

"Sure." Halloran's eyes gleamed. "That's a nice touch, shamus. Make sure you get some of her lipstick on your lips. You can bite her a couple of times, too, if you want to. That'll be the clincher." Halloran laughed wildly. "Yeah, bite her, shamus! Dammit, bite her!"

Max walked slowly to the bed, stopped beside it—and took her hand in his. Her fingers were cold, but they clung gently to his—and she smiled confidently up at him. "Does it still hurt?" she whispered.

"What?" For a moment he didn't understand.

"This is the wounded one, isn't it?" Her fingers pressed his.

"Yeah." He nodded. "Mind if I kiss you, Gwen?"

There were tears in her eyes suddenly, but behind the tears there was a brightness that sent a surge of hope through his heart. "I want you to, darling," she said softly.

He bent down toward her slowly, hearing the silence, feeling the pounding of blood in his veins, sensing the nearness of death—and then he grabbed for the gun. Halloran had been watching them, a sardonic smile on his lips, and Max heard him suck in his breath sharply. In the split second of startlement, Max fired once...heard Halloran's gun explode...and fired again. Max's shoulder began to throb and he saw Halloran spin around and stumble. He heard Gwen's piercing scream and the rattle of shattered glass falling somewhere. And in the same second of nightmarish horror he saw the huge snake slithering through the bathroom doorway, its ugly head erect and seeking and its thick black body undulating rhythmically as it headed swiftly toward them.

Max flung himself over Gwen's struggling body, gained the other side of the bed, and fired twice at the ropes that still bound one of her wrists to a head-post.

Somewhere in the building people were shouting and he could hear them running. Then he had Gwen in his arms and her hands were clutching his neck and he was staggering with her toward the door...

*   *   *

A cool hand was stroking his forehead.

Max moved his lips. "Gwen?" he asked.

"Hush." The hand left his forehead and fingers touched his lips. "You're supposed to go to sleep."

"You're all right?"

"I'm fine, darling." Her voice was as soft and caressing as a kitten's tongue. "You lost a lot of blood and need rest, so let me do the talking. Your shoulder got in the way again. Does it hurt?"

"A little," Max admitted. He opened his eyes and tried to smile. She still wore the torn blouse, but someone had pinned it together for her. Her face was pale and worried-looking—and beautiful. "Halloran?" he asked curiously.

She was silent a moment. Her hand squeezed his. "You didn't kill him. A bullet shattered the glass and the snake got to him, and... I guess he deserved it, though."

He felt her shudder. "The snake?" he asked.

"Sergeant Nehlson killed it. He and a squad of men had the building surrounded and as soon as they heard the shots they started to break in. He thought you were inside, he said, but he wasn't sure. He said he knew that you were worried about me, and that you probably had some scheme for breaking into the apartment there, but he didn't think you were foolish enough to try anything single-handed. They arrested a lot of people—a Mrs. Tangier and two girls and someone named Verne and a man whose name I forgot. Sergeant Nehlson says they were all in cahoots with Halloran and—guess what?"

Max smiled. "What?"

"They found a lot of—what did he call them?—oh, danglers and ice and a couple of lamesters, too, and Sergeant Nehlson says it'll be a long time before any of them do any boosting again. Boosting—that's stealing, isn't it?"

"Yeah."

"Oh, I almost forgot. Verne was padded, he said—whatever that means—and you're going to get a lot of publicity out of all the arrests and maybe a reward, too, if they can find which ice-house got shook, and—"

It required an effort, but Max managed to blow rudely through his lips.

"You don't believe it?" She sounded surprised.

"Nehlson's trying to get kicked upstairs," Max said slowly. He stared at the ceiling. "That line is strictly out of headquarters. Hell, Halloran was a cop."

Puzzlement marred her forehead. "I don't understand, darling—"

"Halloran carried a shield, kiddo, and that's thicker than blood. They figure that if they play me up big, maybe the voters won't notice Halloran's sergeancy sticking out...not that I give a damn, but—"

"You're talking too much, Max. How do you feel?"

"Lousy," He smiled faintly.

"Want anything?"

Max closed his eyes. "Uh-huh."

"What?"

"I never did get that kiss, did I?"

He felt her lips coming closer and closer and his shoulder throbbed and his blood pounded—and it was wonderful.

THE END

If you've enjoyed this book, you will not want to miss these terrific titles…

ARMCHAIR SCIENCE FICTION & MYSTERY CLASSICS, $12.95 each

If you've enjoyed this book, you will not want to miss these terrific titles...

ARMCHAIR SCI-FI & HORROR DOUBLE NOVELS, $12.95 each

D-1   **THE GALAXY RAIDERS** by William P. McGivern
         SPACE STATION #1 by Frank Belknap Long

D-2   **THE PROGRAMMED PEOPLE** by Jack Sharkey
         SLAVES OF THE CRYSTAL BRAIN by William Carter Sawtelle

D-3   **YOU'RE ALL ALONE** by Fritz Leiber
         THE LIQUID MAN by Bernard C. Gilford

D-4   **CITADEL OF THE STAR LORDS** by Edmond Hamilton
         VOYAGE TO ETERNITY by Milton Lesser

D-5   **IRON MEN OF VENUS** by Don Wilcox
         THE MAN WITH ABSOLUTE MOTION by Noel Loomis

D-6   **WHO SOWS THE WIND...** by Rog Phillips
         THE PUZZLE PLANET by Robert A. W. Lowndes

D-7   **PLANET OF DREAD** by Murray Leinster
         TWICE UPON A TIME by Charles L. Fontenay

D-8   **THE TERROR OUT OF SPACE** by Dwight V. Swain
         QUEST OF THE GOLDEN APE by Ivar Jorgensen and Adam Chase

D-9   **SECRET OF MARRACOTT DEEP** by Henry Slesar
         PAWN OF THE BLACK FLEET by Mark Clifton.

D-10   **BEYOND THE RINGS OF SATURN** by Robert Moore Williams
         A MAN OBSESSED by Alan E. Nourse

ARMCHAIR SCIENCE FICTION CLASSICS, $12.95 each

C-1   **THE GREEN MAN**
         by Harold M. Sherman

C-2   **A TRACE OF MEMORY**
         By Keith Laumer

C-3   **INTO PLUTONIAN DEPTHS**
         by Stanton A. Coblentz

ARMCHAIR MASTERS OF SCIENCE FICTION SERIES, $16.95 each

M-1   **MASTERS OF SCIENCE FICTION, Vol. One**
         Bryce Walton—"Dark of the Moon" and other tales

M-2   **MASTERS OF SCIENCE FICTION, Vol. Two**
         Jerome Bixby—"One Way Street" and other tales

If you've enjoyed this book, you will not want to miss these terrific titles…

ARMCHAIR SCI-FI & HORROR DOUBLE NOVELS, $12.95 each

D-11   **PERIL OF THE STARMEN** by Kris Neville
THE STRANGE INVASION by Murray Leinster

D-12   **THE STAR LORD** by Boyd Ellanby
CAPTIVES OF THE FLAME by Samuel R. Delany

D-13   **MEN OF THE MORNING STAR** by Edmond Hamilton
PLANET FOR PLUNDER by Hal Clement and Sam Merwin, Jr.

D-14   **ICE CITY OF THE GORGON** by Chester S. Geier and Richard Shaver
WHEN THE WORLD TOTTERED by Lester del Rey

D-15   **WORLDS WITHOUT END** by Clifford D. Simak
THE LAVENDER VINE OF DEATH by Don Wilcox

D-16   **SHADOW ON THE MOON** by Joe Gibson
ARMAGEDDON EARTH by Geoff St. Reynard

D-17   **THE GIRL WHO LOVED DEATH** by Paul W. Fairman
SLAVE PLANET by Laurence M. Janifer

D-18   **SECOND CHANCE** by J. F. Bone
MISSION TO A DISTANT STAR by Frank Belknap Long

D-19   **THE SYNDIC** by C. M. Kornbluth
FLIGHT TO FOREVER by Poul Anderson

D-20   **SOMEWHERE I'LL FIND YOU** by Milton Lesser
THE TIME ARMADA by Fox B. Holden

ARMCHAIR SCIENCE FICTION CLASSICS, $12.95 each

C-4   **CORPUS EARTHLING**
by Louis Charbonneau

C-5   **THE TIME DISSOLVER**
by Jerry Sohl

C-6   **WEST OF THE SUN**
by Edgar Pangborn

ARMCHAIR SCI-FI & HORROR GEMS SERIES, $12.95 each

G-1   **SCIENCE FICTION GEMS, Vol. One**
Isaac Asimov and others

G-2   **HORROR GEMS, Vol. One**
Carl Jacobi and others

If you've enjoyed this book, you will not want to miss these terrific titles...

ARMCHAIR SCI-FI & HORROR DOUBLE NOVELS, $12.95 each

ARMCHAIR SCIENCE FICTION CLASSICS, $12.95 each

ARMCHAIR SCI-FI & HORROR GEMS SERIES, $12.95 each

If you've enjoyed this book, you will not want to miss these terrific titles…

ARMCHAIR SCI-FI & HORROR DOUBLE NOVELS, $12.95 each

D-41   **FULL CYCLE** by Clifford D. Simak
\   **IT WAS THE DAY OF THE ROBOT** by Frank Belknap Long

D-42   **THIS CROWDED EARTH** by Robert Bloch
            REIGN OF THE TELEPUPPETS by Daniel Galouye

D-43   **THE CRISPIN AFFAIR** by Jack Sharkey
            THE RED HELL OF JUPITER by Paul Ernst

D-44   **PLANET OF DREAD** by Dwight V. Swain
            WE THE MACHINE by Gerald Vance

D-45   **THE STAR HUNTER** by Edmond Hamilton
            THE ALIEN by Raymond F. Jones

D-46   **WORLD OF IF** by Rog Phillips
            SLAVE RAIDERS FROM MERCURY by Don Wilcox

D-47   **THE ULTIMATE PERIL** by Robert Abernathy
            PLANET OF SHAME by Bruce Elliot

D-48   **THE FLYING EYES** by J. Hunter Holly
            SOME FABULOUS YONDER by Phillip Jose Farmer

D-49   **THE COSMIC BUNGLARS** by Geoff St. Reynard
            THE BUTTONED SKY by Geoff St. Reynard

D-50   **TYRANTS OF TIME** by Milton Lesser
            PARIAH PLANET by Murray Leinster

ARMCHAIR SCIENCE FICTION CLASSICS, $12.95 each

C-13   **SUNKEN WORLD**
            by Stanton A. Coblentz

C-14   **THE LAST VIAL**
            by Sam McClatchie, M. D.

C-15   **WE WHO SURVIVED (THE FIFTH ICE AGE)**
            by Sterling Noel

ARMCHAIR MASTERS OF SCIENCE FICTION SERIES, $16.95 each

MS-5   **MASTERS OF SCIENCE FICTION, Vol. Five**
            Winston K. Marks—Test Colony and other tales

MS-6   **MASTERS OF SCIENCE FICTION, Vol. Six**
            Fritz Leiber—Deadly Moon and other tales

If you've enjoyed this book, you will not want to miss these terrific titles...

ARMCHAIR SCI-FI & HORROR DOUBLE NOVELS, $12.95 each

D-51   **A GOD NAMED SMITH** by Henry Slesar
       WORLDS OF THE IMPERIUM by Keith Laumer

D-52   **CRAIG'S BOOK** by Don Wilcox
       EDGE OF THE KNIFE by H. Beam Piper

D-53   **THE SHINING CITY** by Rena M. Vale
       THE RED PLANET by Russ Winterbotham

D-54   **THE MAN WHO LIVED TWICE** by Rog Phillips
       VALLEY OF THE CROEN by Lee Tarbell

D-55   **OPERATION DISASTER** by Milton Lesser
       LAND OF THE DAMNED by Berkeley Livingston

D-56   **CAPTIVE OF THE CENTAURIANESS** by Poul Anderson
       A PRINCESS OF MARS by Edgar Rice Burroughs

D-57   **THE NON-STATISTICAL MAN** by Raymond F. Jones
       MISSION FROM MARS by Rick Conroy

D-58   **INTRUDERS FROM THE STARS** by Ross Rocklynne
       FLIGHT OF THE STARLING by Chester S. Geier

D-59   **COSMIC SABOTEUR** by Frank M. Robinson
       LOOK TO THE STARS by Willard Hawkins

D-60   **THE MOON IS HELL!** by John W. Campbell, Jr.
       THE GREEN WORLD by Hal Clement

ARMCHAIR SCIENCE FICTION CLASSICS, $12.95 each

C-16   **THE SHAVER MYSTERY, Book Three**
       by Richard S. Shaver

C-17   **THE PLANET STRAPPERS**
       by Raymond Z. Gallun

C-18   **THE FOURTH "R"**
       by George O. Smith

ARMCHAIR SCI-FI & HORROR GEMS SERIES, $12.95 each

G-5   **SCIENCE FICTION GEMS, Vol. Three**
       C. M. Kornbluth and others

G-6   **HORROR GEMS, Vol. Three**
       August Derleth and others

If you've enjoyed this book, you will not want to miss these terrific titles...

ARMCHAIR SCI-FI & HORROR DOUBLE NOVELS, $12.95 each

D-61 **THE MAN WHO STOPPED AT NOTHING** by Paul W. Fairman
TEN FROM INFINITY by Ivar Jorgensen

D-62 **WORLDS WITHIN** by Rog Phillips
THE SLAVE by C.M. Kornbluth

D-63 **SECRET OF THE BLACK PLANET** by Milton Lesser
THE OUTCASTS OF SOLAR III by Emmett McDowell

D-64 **WEB OF THE WORLDS** by Harry Harrison and Katherine MacLean
RULE GOLDEN by Damon Knight

D-65 **TEN TO THE STARS** by Raymond Z. Gallun
THE CONQUERORS by David H. Keller, M. D.

D-66 **THE HORDE FROM INFINITY** by Dwight V. Swain
THE DAY THE EARTH FROZE by Gerald Hatch

D-67 **THE WAR OF THE WORLDS** by H. G. Wells
THE TIME MACHINE by H. G. Wells

D-68 **STARCOMBERS** by Edmond Hamilton
THE YEAR WHEN STARDUST FELL by Raymond F. Jones

D-69 **HOCUS-POCUS UNIVERSE** by Jack Williamson
QUEEN OF THE PANTHER WORLD by Berkeley Livingston

D-70 **BATTERING RAMS OF SPACE** by Don Wilcox
DOOMSDAY WING by George H. Smith

ARMCHAIR SCIENCE FICTION CLASSICS, $12.95 each

C-19 **EMPIRE OF JEGGA**
by David V. Reed

C-20 **THE TOMORROW PEOPLE**
by Judith Merril

C-21 **THE MAN FROM YESTERDAY**
by Howard Browne as by Lee Francis

C-22 **THE TIME TRADERS**
by Andre Norton

C-23 **ISLANDS OF SPACE**
by John W. Campbell

C-24 **THE GALAXY PRIMES**
by E. E. "Doc" Smith

If you've enjoyed this book, you will not want to miss these terrific titles...

ARMCHAIR SCI-FI & HORROR DOUBLE NOVELS, $12.95 each

D-71 **THE DEEP END** by Gregory Luce
TO WATCH BY NIGHT by Robert Moore Williams

D-72 **SWORDSMAN OF LOST TERRA** by Poul Anderson
PLANET OF GHOSTS by David V. Reed

D-73 **MOON OF BATTLE** by J. J. Allerton
THE MUTANT WEAPON by Murray Leinster

D-74 **OLD SPACEMEN NEVER DIE!** John Jakes
RETURN TO EARTH by Bryan Berry

D-75 **THE THING FROM UNDERNEATH** by Milton Lesser
OPERATION INTERSTELLAR by George O. Smith

D-76 **THE BURNING WORLD** by Algis Budrys
FOREVER IS TOO LONG by Chester S. Geier

D-77 **THE COSMIC JUNKMAN** by Rog Phillips
THE ULTIMATE WEAPON by John W. Campbell

D-78 **THE TIES OF EARTH** by James H. Schmitz
CUE FOR QUIET by Thomas L. Sherred

D-79 **SECRET OF THE MARTIANS** by Paul W. Fairman
THE VARIABLE MAN by Philip K. Dick

D-80 **THE GREEN GIRL** by Jack Williamson
THE ROBOT PERIL by Don Wilcox

ARMCHAIR SCIENCE FICTION CLASSICS, $12.95 each

C-25 **THE STAR KINGS**
by Edmond Hamilton

C-26 **NOT IN SOLITUDE**
by Kenneth Gantz

C-32 **PROMETHEUS II**
by S. J. Byrne

ARMCHAIR SCI-FI & HORROR GEMS SERIES, $12.95 each

G-7 **SCIENCE FICTION GEMS, Vol. Seven**
Jack Sharkey and others

G-8 **HORROR GEMS, Vol. Eight**
Seabury Quinn and others